CLEAN-UP TIME

Francisco Braun was unhappy because he wasn't allowed to kill Remo and Chiun and the woman himself. Especially the woman. Braun adored women, alive and then dead.

But the golden-haired assassin had his orders, and he unleashed the swarm of murderous thugs against the three down in their isolated cabin. Minutes later, Braun was puzzled. No gunfire, no screams. Then from his hiding place Braun saw Chiun growl an order at Remo and heard Remo complain, "If you kill them, you should clean them up. There are large garbage bags in the kitchen. You can get them as well as anyone." Still muttering, Remo piled up the bodies of Braun's assault force in neat stacks by the kitchen door.

Then a smile came to Francisco Braun's incredibly handsome face. Clearly these targets were worthy of his own very special skills. . . .

—THE DESTROYER #64—

THE LAST ALCHEMIST

More Classic Novels of Suspense from Warren Murphy
& Richard Sapir

#64

The Destroyer

THE LAST ALCHEMIST

WARREN MURPHY & RICHARD SAPIR

A SIGNET BOOK

NEW AMERICAN LIBRARY

NAL BOOKS ARE AVAILABLE AT QUANTITY DISCOUNTS WHEN USED TO PROMOTE
PRODUCTS OR SERVICES. FOR INFORMATION PLEASE WRITE TO PREMIUM
MARKETING DIVISION, NEW AMERICAN LIBRARY, 1633 BROADWAY,
NEW YORK, NEW YORK 10019.

SIGNET TRADEMARK REG. U.S.PAT. OFF. AND FOREIGN COUNTRIES
REGISTERED TRADEMARK—MARCA REGISTRADA
HECHO EN CHICAGO, U.S.A.

Signet, Signet Classic, Mentor, Plume, Meridian and NAL Books
are published by New American Library,
1633 Broadway, New York, New York 10019

First Printing, April, 1986

1 2 3 4 5 6 7 8 9

PRINTED IN THE UNITED STATES OF AMERICA

For Richard and Carolyn Senier,
who make music of their lives

1

The bodies were still there, preserved by the cold and dark of the sea, just as he said they would be. And they were right where he said they'd find them: two hundred feet down, off the coast of Spain, in the belly of a Spanish man-of-war. Maneuvering in the slow dream-walk of the deep, the diver moved around the open hatch, watching the pantaloons of the dead quiver in the currents created with his heavy leaded feet. They were Spanish soldiers of the king, he had been told, guarding the ship for eternity. They would not harm him, he had been told. He had answered that he wasn't afraid of the dead; he was afraid of the old diving suit he had to wear. If they did find the wreck, and he had to enter it, an air hose going up to the mother ship could get caught in one of the old timbers.

"You're not getting paid to test modern equipment, you're getting paid to find a damned ship and get me something," Mr. Harrison Caldwell had told him from behind a desk in a very modern salvage office in Barcelona. Mr. Caldwell was an American, but strangely he could speak Spanish as though born a grandee. The diver, Jésus Gómez, had been warned of that, warned

not to make little snide remarks about the gringo in
Spanish.

"Mr. Caldwell, sir. There is no amount of money that
is worth my life, sir," Jésus Gómez had answered. He
made his protest about the old air hose in practiced
English. Jésus was the son and grandson of divers, men
who had gone under the water for sponges without any
equipment and ended up crippled from the bends,
walking into old age stooped like ships heeling to one
side. He knew that if he wished to walk upright for the
rest of his life, he would have to dive with equipment.
Getting equipment meant not diving for sponges but
things under the sea important people wanted. And
important people meant English-speaking people. So
Jésus, the diver, learned English early on. The first word
Jésus Gómez learned was "mister." The second was
"sir."

"Mr. Caldwell, sir. If I lose my life, what good is
money? There is not enough money, sir, to pay for my
life," Jésus Gómez had told Mr. Caldwell.

"Oh, there most certainly is," Harrison Caldwell had
said, brushing something imaginary off his dark
immaculate suit. "Let's not waste time in this infernal
Latin bargaining. Everything has a price; people are just
too stupid to know it. Now, we are not talking about
your definite death. We are talking about a risk of
death."

"Yessir," said Jésus Gómez. He sat a bit more stiffly
than normal, because his mouth had learned the words,
but not his soul.

"You risk your life every time you go down, so we are
not even negotiating the risk of your life, but how much
of a risk."

"That is correct, Mr. Caldwell."

"Therefore, what is your price for the greater risk?"

"Sir, may I ask why you insist on the old air line connected to a heavy steel helmet and a diving suit? Air lines get tangled in wrecks. Suits are heavy. Wrecks are dangerous enough without entering them on the end of a thin air line."

"I wish to have contact all the time. I wish to have telephone contact all the time."

"Sir, may I suggest the new scuba equipment for me, with a telephone line for you. I will be safe. You will have your diving service, and we will both be happy."

"My way, fifteen thousand dollars for the week," said Harrison Caldwell. He had a sharp long face with a high-bridged nose, and an imperious dark-eyed stare that always reminded others of what, exactly, Harrison Caldwell thought they were—servants.

"Sir, I will do it for ten thousand, but let me use my own gear."

"Thirty thousand. We use mine," said Harrison Caldwell.

"Sir . . ."

"Forty," said Mr. Caldwell.

"Fifty," said Jésus Gómez, and when the American agreed so readily, Jésus Gómez cursed himself for not demanding more. But still, fifty thousand American dollars, for one week of diving, was more than his father had made in a lifetime. Though Jésus was a man of twenty-eight, he almost did not tell his father of his good fortune; Jésus feared his father might regret his having given up his life for so little.

"Jésus," said his father, "fifty thousand dollars American is far too much for a week of diving. It is too much."

"There is no such thing as too much."

"There is always a thing that is too much," said the father. "I am afraid I will never see you again."

"You will see me rich, Father. You will see a new home, and the good wine bought in bottles, and American cigarettes, and the French cheeses you once had on your trip to the big city. And Mama will have lace for her hair."

"Too much for one week," his father had said. But his father was an old man who was crippled at forty from diving without any gear for the sponges that became farther and farther out, deeper and deeper down. An old man who had spent his strong days earning in his entire life the equivalent of twelve thousand American dollars.

And so Jésus Gómez had taken the dive, and as Mr. Caldwell had said, the ship was waiting for him, including the dead men.

"Yes, Mr. Caldwell," said Jésus Gómez, activating the telephone line with a switch. "I see the bodies where you said they would be."

"Good," said Mr. Caldwell. "Are they wearing pantaloons?"

"Yessir, Mr. Caldwell."

"That is the front hatch, then. Go to the stern. I will wait."

Slowly Jésus Gómez made his way along the dark planking of the ship, shining the special deep light ahead of his steps, careful not to put his full weight on any plank lest he fall into the hull. Small fish darted in the bright beam, a hole of light in the great darkness of the silent deep. The wood was intact but not strong, not after more than four hundred years. When he reached the stern hatch, his light picked up white skulls, piled like cannonballs in a pyramid.

"Santa Maria," gasped Jésus Gómez.

"You're there," came down Harrison Caldwell's

voice. "Wait for the camera." Even two hundred feet down, Jesus could see the strong lights break the surface above. By the time the lights were within the reach of his hands, they were blinding. He had to shut his eyes and grope. Once he had them pointed away, he saw they were mounted on a still camera, a very large still camera, strangely large considering that a movie camera would have been half the size.

"Leave the skulls where they are," came Mr. Caldwell's voice. "Let yourself and the camera down, carefully down, on the prow side of the skulls. You will be walking toward the center."

"I am afraid of my air."

"You have twenty more minutes of work to do to collect the rest of your fifty thousand. Come, come. You are not really in a negotiating position."

When Jésus Gómez shone the light into the dark hull with ribbing torn from the capsizing that took place centuries before, the words "sir" and "mister" came very slow from his throat. But they came nevertheless. Always mindful of his air line, he called for more, and pulled it in a loose coil to his side, careful to avoid a crimp. He would know when he had a crimp. He simply wouldn't be able to breathe.

With the coil carefully at his side, he allowed himself to fall slowly into the hull, prayers on his lips all the way.

It was an insane way to dive, he knew. The camera came with him, its lights making sunshine on wood turned coal black by centuries of the Atlantic. His weighted diving boots kicked a bar and the bar did not move. Heavier than lead. He shone the light down, and it was what he suspected. Gold. A bar of gold. No, tons of gold, piled along the entire length and width of the hull, stacked like cordwood in some peasant's hut. No wonder Mr. Caldwell so easily agreed to fifty thousand dollars.

"Do you want me to photograph your gold now, Mr. Caldwell, sir?" said Jésus Gómez, the words now a joy because he knew why the money could be so plentiful. He was no longer obsessed with the danger of the dive, but with the richness of it.

"No, no. Forget the gold. Farther toward the prow you will find it."

"A man who does not value gold, a ship guarded by skulls."

"Gómez, I value gold more than anything. As for guarding by skulls, that was an old practice for treasure. One skull per fortune."

"But there is a stack of skulls back there."

"Yes," said Mr. Caldwell.

"What should I photograph?"

"You will see it. You cannot miss it. It is made of stone, simple black basalt. And it is round."

"Just that, sir?"

"That's what you are being paid for," came back the voice of Mr. Caldwell.

At that moment the air became just a bit more difficult to breathe, and not because of the line. Jésus was very careful about that line, jiggling it free from above and behind him every few feet, careful of the insurance coil of slack. At the first resistance of the line, he pulled no more and used the coil. He would not, he vowed, go one step beyond that coil.

If there was gold in the stern, stacks of it, then there has to be more of it for ballast, he thought. Unless, of course, the stone is the ballast. The big stone in the middle of the ship is the ballast.

And then he thought some more, stepping carefully

over the floating hand of a man whose sword had been useless to defend his life under the water.

No, he thought. If I am to photograph the stone, then the gold is the ballast. The stone had to be the many treasures, the reason for the many skulls. Such was the stunning revelation that came to Jésus Gómez as he stumbled onto the stone. It hit his feet. It was round, almost a perfect circle the diameter of a short man.

"I have found it."

"Turn on the camera. There is a rubber plunger switch at the rear . . . good. That's it. Don't kick up the mud." This from Mr. Caldwell, who could obviously see through this camera. But that did not explain why it was so large. Television cameras could be made as small as a loaf of bread.

"There are four quadrants," said Mr. Caldwell. "Do you see them?"

"Oh, yes," said Gómez. The stone was divided into four parts. In the days of the Spanish, gold coins were divided into pieces of eight, and quarters, where the modern Americans got the name of their silver pieces from, not from quarters of dollars as they liked to believe.

"Stand on the edge of the closest quadrant."

"Yes, Mr. Caldwell."

"Point the camera directly at your feet, and hold the camera steady."

"I am, Mr. Caldwell."

"Press the button on your left."

"I am doing that, Mr. Caldwell." Jésus felt the camera whir and felt little clicks. Jésus did that two times minimum for every section of the quadrant, sometimes doing it as many as five times. And by this he realized every picture he took was seen and recorded on the surface ship, because otherwise Mr. Caldwell would not know to ask for another picture unless he could see something he didn't like in the first ones.

Jésus thought he recognized some of the letters but could read no language. There were Arabic letters, he thought. Spanish letters, he thought. But the words were not Spanish, even though he thought he recognized one or two.

Perhaps, he thought while waiting for the camera to do its job, one language is Latin. I have seen words like this chiseled into church walls. Perhaps the Arabic is old, too, he thought. Other letters he could not even remotely recognize.

As he checked his watch he realized that if he had taken down tanks he would not have been able to stay so long. This made him feel better. There was some logic now to the risky suit. Mr. Caldwell wanted his photographs done in one dive. It would be fifty thousand dollars for a day. He had done all four quadrants. There was nothing left to do. He waited for Mr. Caldwell to call him up to the surface. Finally, he could wait no longer.

"Are we done, Mr. Caldwell?" said Jésus Gómez.

There was no answer from above. He felt his ears ring. Something was pushing in on his skull. The breathing was hard, like his lungs were being pushed out into his rib cage. It was hot, very hot for this deep. Then he realized the air pressure in the suit was increasing. Becoming enormous. He tried to move across the planking but his weighted feet were rising. He was rising. And he couldn't stop it.

"Mr. Caldwell, Mr. Caldwell. Lower the pressure. Lower the pressure," cried Jésus Gómez. He felt himself lift from the base of the hull, rising toward the upper decks. The underside of the deck felt strangely soft. Very soft. It was as though the ceiling was as springy and as pliable as a balloon. Then he saw it—a gloved hand in

a bloated arm. The pressure had pushed him into
another diver, a diver who was also pinned to the roof.
Dangling from the diver's hand was a camera similar to
the one Mr. Caldwell had given Jésus, except it had a
single light. Jésus had been sent a strong battery of
lights. Did they try the first time and find out there were
not enough lights to photograph the stone? But why did
they strand the diver? At that moment, pinned inside the
wreck of a ship two hundred feet and four centuries
beneath the surface, Jésus Gómez knew exactly why Mr.
Caldwell was willing to pay fifty thousand dollars for a
week. He would have paid fifty million for a week.
Because Mr. Caldwell never intended to pay him at all.
Mr. Caldwell paid only in air pressure.

Jésus saw the air line and the camera line float away.
Apparently they could disassemble them from above,
plugging the air line at Jésus' end. He knew it was from
his end because bubbles came from the retreating end
like a snake, like a snake of life saying good-bye to Jésus
Gómez pinned to the ceiling of an old ship, another skull
to guard the many treasures. He wondered if he should
cut open his suit, just to get free of the ceiling. Of course
he would drown, but maybe he could somehow get to
that bubbling hose going away, taunting him with the air
he needed. But the arms of Jésus Gómez, trapped in a
taut balloon of a suit, could not move. And besides, the
pressure was turning everything black anyhow. Or was
it the batteries going out in the lights? Could they turn
those out from above? he wondered. His father had been
right. It was too much money. And his last dim thoughts
as his body gave up its quest for air, in the warm
comforting narcotic of death, was that his father, the
poor sponge diver, was right. Too much money. Too
much.

Professor Augustine Cryx of Brussels had to laugh. Not only was it too much money, but anyone willing to pay money at all for his services had to be suspect.

"What? Calling from America? Is there something wrong with the postal service? Eh? I can't hear you."

"Professor Cryx, this is a perfect telephone connection. And you're hearing well. I want you to look at several photographs tomorrow. I will pay whatever you ask, just see me tomorrow."

Professor Cryx laughed. Even the laughter was old, almost a crackle coming from a dry throat. He was eighty-seven years old, lived a life of virtual obscurity, pensioned off by the university in quiet embarrassment after the Second World War, and now someone was offering him four times what his yearly salary had been just to look at some pictures.

"Mr. Caldwell," said Professor Cryx. "What would I do with the money? I have no need of money. How many years do you think I have left?"

"What do you want?" said Harrison Caldwell. "Name it."

"I wish to enjoy the feast of St. Vincense D'Ors. And that is tomorrow. And I have my wine, and I make libations in all four corners of the world, and chant the words so dear to his heart."

"I can build a statue for him or of him, Professor Cryx. I'll make a donation to the church in St. Vincense D'Ors' name."

"Wouldn't do any good, Mr. Caldwell. The Roman Catholic Church cleared poor Vincense out with St. Christopher and Philomena and so many others, years ago. We all no longer belong, including me. We are all finished and done with. Good day, Mr. Caldwell."

"Wait. I can make a donation to the Catholic Church. They serve the living. I'll build them hospitals in St.

Vincense's name. That's what you can do for St. Vincense D'Ors if you see me tomorrow. The Church won't turn down helping the poor.''

Again there was laughter over the transatlantic line. ''Mr. Caldwell. Good old St. Vincense needs his libations and holy words. He needs them here in Brussels where he was born. Now why are you offering me so much money for a discredited science, so discredited that even in my youth I was forced to teach it as the history of the medieval ages? Why?''

''Let me ask you then, sir. Why are you so insistent on performing those ceremonies tomorrow? Why not let others do it?''

''Because, Mr. Caldwell, I am the only one to pour libations on St. Vincense's birthday. I am the last.''

''I will carry it on.''

''You lie. What do you care about the patron saint of alchemy? The science has been discredited for over a century. But I tell you, the alchemists were the beginning of Western science, no matter what you or anyone else says. No matter what the university feels. Other sciences have flaws. Do they call physics superstition because a theory doesn't work? Do they call psychoanalysis superstition because someone comes up with a new definition of the id? No. But alchemy, the source of Western chemistry and science, was discarded entirely as a superstition just because a few theories did not prove out.''

''Why are you yelling, professor? If I didn't believe, would I be offering to pay you so much money for one day?''

Harrison Caldwell heard heavy breathing at the other end of the line. The man might be having a stroke. He had to gentle him down, not antagonize him.

''I am tired of being ridiculed. Leave me alone.''

"I have something that you must believe in," said Caldwell.

"I don't have to believe in anything. I don't have to believe the world isn't composed of the four pure elements of fire, water, earth, and air. I don't have to. And I will tell you something else, you . . . you mocker of our science. I never will."

"I have the philosopher's stone," said Harrison Caldwell.

"If I were to believe you, I would be even more offended. That stone. Always, always the problem. They said that because we claimed as alchemists to be able to turn lead to gold, we were a pseudoscience, the court jesters of science, the embarrassment of science, like an old grandfather born bastard instead of legal. But this bastard made your chemists of today, son."

"The stone is in four quadrants. Two of the languages I recognize. They are Latin and Arabic. The third might be a form of Greek, but I am not sure, and, Professor Cryx, I dreadfully hate talking about this on a telephone line. What sort of wine do we pour to St. Vincense D'Ors?"

There was a pause on the telephone line. Finally Professor Cryx spoke.

"It's a long ceremony. I have been using a cheap port, but you do have funds, you say?"

"What sort of wine would our blessed St. Vincense like?"

The voice from Brussels was timid, almost like a child unable to believe it was worth such a gift.

"Laffite Rothschild . . . if it isn't too expensive."

"We will have two cases for Blessed St. Vincense. A hundred if you wish."

"Too much, too much. But yes, of course. Wine is one of the few pleasures of the old. A hundred cases would allow me to drink every day for the rest of my life. Oh this is too good, too good to be true. You will be here tomorrow then. Services start at sunrise."

The next day, Harrison Caldwell saw clearly why the Church never recognized good old St. Vincense. Half the prayers were pagan, and the other half were pagan-based, calling upon the elements as though they were gods themselves. The ritual was anathema to the first of the Ten Commandments, which called for reverence to one God who made everything.

Professor Cryx was a Walloon, one of the two groups that made up Belgium, and the one that usually ran things. The other group, the Flemish, only felt it should run things. Professor Cryx wore a gray jacket stained by all the meals he'd eaten since middle age. They stood in an old square near an old fountain, while Professor Cryx chanted a language Harrison Caldwell had never heard but suspected might be on one of the four quadrants of the stone. The old man was sparing with the wine, commenting to his St. Vincense that when the other hundred cases arrived there would be more wine. The wine was poured into the fountain. Some of the prayers were in English for Caldwell's benefit. Harrison Caldwell did not bother to mention that he spoke both Dutch and French, which would have enabled him to converse with anyone in Belgium. Nor did he mention that he spoke Spanish, ancient Greek, Latin, Russian, Chinese, Arabic, Hebrew, and Danish.

Nor did he even mention that he spoke all of these languages fluently, like someone who used them daily. Harrison Caldwell stood with the grace and tremendous reserve of someone who was sure that in a very short time he was going to realize a dream of generations.

With casual ease, Harrison Caldwell allowed an arm to gently rest on a hip. Oddly, this small gesture attracted a crowd. The sight of a ragged old man pouring wine into a fountain and mumbling things in one language after another aroused only pity, making people turn away. But to see someone so elegant stand there with the old man, as though about to receive a crown of a kingdom, was something to make people stop and look. And when Professor Cryx bowed four times to the four corners of the world, praising the four elements for their gifts as St. Vincense D'Ors had taught, people came over to ask what the ceremony was about.

"We're getting followers," gasped Professor Cryx.

"Move on," said Caldwell. And they did. Not just because the elegant man ignored all requests as though he had never heard them, but because when Harrison Caldwell did not respond to people he made them feel ashamed that they had ever spoken. He had that ability with employees, even from his earliest days when he had to work for a living. But those days would soon be over.

The professor's apartment was small, dim, and smelled like an unopened trash barrel. But the old professor was giddy with joy; a second life had begun even as his days dwindled. He was talking of plans, something he hadn't indulged in since the 1960s when alchemy made a very brief comeback on the coattails of the astronomy craze. Harrison Caldwell endured the smell and the conversational discomfort. Then, from a very thin briefcase, he brought forth four pictures. Each showed a quadrant of the stone in harsh clarity. Harrison Caldwell cleared a table for Professor Cryx and poured a glass of wine.

Cryx trembled the glass to his lips, letting the pure sharp wine pleasure his tongue for a delicious moment, finally swallowing almost with regret. Then a full sip, and then a swallow, and then he offered the glass for more.

"You did say we're getting a hundred cases, didn't you?"

"For the rest of your life. The pictures."

"Yes, the pictures. Just a touch there, thank you," said Cryx, making sure the bottle filled the glass. "I guess I can get used to this." His glass full, he returned to the pictures. He held the glass up for another sip while he read the Arabic. The Latin was clear. The Arabic was not, and then the ancient Hebrew, the one even before the language of the Old Testament. And of course Sanskrit. Good old Sanskrit. The Babylonian variation. The glass stayed where he had placed it. He didn't even notice Mr. Caldwell, the nice Mr. Caldwell, take it out of his hands.

"Yes. Yes. Of course. Yes. This is it. The old devil himself. Where did you find it?"

"It was sunk."

"Leave it there. This has caused us alchemists the trouble, all the trouble, from day one. This one stone has been the defamation of us all. Leave it. If you believe in alchemy, leave this stone."

"The one that shows how to turn lead into gold."

"The one that led us to be called frauds and hoaxers. If it weren't for this stone, our cures for the blains and rheumy would have been given the prominence they deserve. Our formulas and beliefs would have survived most respected. Instead our work was stolen from us, given the name of chemistry, and credited to the thieves. Leave the stone be. Alchemists are not mere goldmakers, and never were."

"But what if the stone is true? What if the great lie were shown to be the great truth?"

"I have asked myself many times that same question, Mr. Caldwell, and the sad answer is that the stone was our one lie. And we paid for it dearly. For you, sir, are looking at the last alchemist. And that stone is the reason."

"But it is true."

"No. If it were true, would we not have been rich?"

"Not necessarily."

"Why not? Don't tease me like this. Please, tell me. Why not?"

"Because you don't know gold," said Harrison Caldwell. "I left what would be calculated today at perhaps twelve million American dollars at the bottom of the sea because I know gold. I know what it does. I know what it feels like. I know you think it is the noble metal. The most noble metal."

"Yes. I do. Alchemists have always called it the noble metal."

"I left twelve million dollars of it on the bottom of the sea, because it is like a speck, a pathetic speck compared to this stone."

"Go back and get your gold, Mr. Caldwell," said Professor Cryx, looking for his glass again, the one with the exquisite wine. He found it and took a hard gulp of it, shaking his head. "If we could have turned lead to gold, then we would have. We would have saved our lives, I tell you. How many of us were beheaded or burned to death when a king placed a pile of lead in front of us and then ordered us at the pain of our lives to produce gold from it? Do you think we would have rather died than do it? Leave the stone. It has been our curse throughout the ages."

"What if I told you I am sure someone did change the lead to gold?"

"You mean the gold you left on the bottom of the

sea?'' asked Professor Cryx. Who was this man who seemed so much like a stranger and yet knew so much about alchemy? One would have thought he would have known the languages.

"As I told you," said Harrison Caldwell, "I know gold. I doubt that gold was made through the formula of the stone. Maybe no more than a few ounces were made in all history by the stone. But if you know gold, and I do know gold, Professor Cryx, you would know why."

"You must tell me. Tell me."

"The answer lies in this stone itself and what I know you—an alchemist—can tell me. You see, gold is really a very plentiful metal. Quite plentiful. In every little cubic mile of seawater there is at least ninety thousand dollars' worth. Did you know that?"

"No. I didn't."

"But it would cost four million dollars to extract it. You see it is uneconomical. There is an economy to gold."

"So it might have taken diamonds to make gold. Something even purer in the fire of the earth," said Professor Cryx.

"No," said Caldwell. "Nothing is purer than gold, or more serviceable, or serving. Or more tradable."

"Then what is it?"

"Obviously something they did not have access to easily."

"What?"

"That is why I am here. Who else can read the old alchemic symbols but you?"

"Of course," said Professor Cryx, putting down the wine again. Mr. Caldwell brought him a pad and pencil, and kept pouring drinks. There was the old symbol for lead, Professor Cryx saw. It was like an old friend. And there was red sulfur. And mercury. A great element was

mercury. Hard to come by, but not unavailable in
history. Only in the old Sanskrit did the descriptions
start to fit. Then Mr. Caldwell was writing furiously on
his own piece of paper. He seemed a bit lax with the
proper chants. But when the Sanskrit yielded the
missing element, Harrison Caldwell said:

"Of course. It would have been very scarce then."

It may have been the amount Professor Cryx was
happily drinking, but the wine suddenly had a giddy
sting to it. Rather nice, but darkening.

"Perhaps I have had enough," said Professor Cryx,
thinking that it might be a nice time to perform a little
prayer of gratitude to the gold itself, asking its power
and spirit to bless their venture, thanking it for the
rebirth of the one true science, soon to be resurrected in
the world, like astronomy and plant worship.

"I'll have a million cases here by your doorstep," said
the wonderful Mr. Caldwell.

A million cases? Was there that much of this fine wine
in the world? It was, after all, just one vineyard.
Professor Cryx thought he was telling this to the nice
Mr. Caldwell, but his tongue was not moving. It was
numb. So were his lips, and so was his body. But it
wasn't until he felt the burning in his stomach that he
recognized the old alchemist's formula for cyanide at
work in its most biting and painful form. When the pain
ended, the old professor was not quite there to feel it
fully. His body was stiff, and only the fingers moved
briefly when the photographs were yanked from under
his hand.

What luck, thought Harrison Caldwell. As his
family had always said, "Spill enough bowels onto the
pavement and the whole city will love you." Which, of
course, was another way of saying he who dared, won.

He left the apartment through the rear and walked out

the alley whistling, whistling a song whose rhythms had not been heard in these city streets for centuries.

Harrison Caldwell not only knew gold, he also knew he would have more of it now than any king since Croesus. And, come to think of it, even more than Croesus ever had. More than anyone, ever. Because Harrison Caldwell knew that nowadays, what the old alchemists lacked was more plentiful than at any other time in history. All one had to do was steal it.

2

His name was Remo and he was supposed to let the little girl drown. The mother was hysterical. As bystanders lined the shores, one young man attempted to get out to her; when he went under he had to be dragged out himself.

It was early spring in Michigan and the ponds were barely covered with cellophane-thin coats of ice. A young girl who had throughout the winter played safely on that ice had fallen through now. It was a pond for summer folk mainly, and the boats, somehow, were all carted away to winter homes. So there she was with no one able to reach her, and a local television camera whirring away. And Remo was supposed to turn and walk away because his picture would be seen on television if he swam through thin ice to save the girl. That would be big news because people could not ordinarily swim through ice.

The television newswoman pushed the microphone into the mother's face.

"How does it feel to watch your daughter drown? Is this your first daughter to drown?" asked the newswoman. Her makeup was camera-perfect. Her hair blew dramatically in the breeze. Remo had seen her on television a few times. They announced she had won an award for reporting. Remo never saw her do anything but read dramatically. He had seen similar situations around the country, in the places he stayed that would never be home. Pretty people would read things into the camera, and then they would collect rewards and be called reporters. Sometimes they thought of things to read all by themselves. Those instances were obvious because a look of desperation crossed their faces, as if it were a struggle to think of an entire word. A complete sentence seemed insurmountable.

The mother's answer was a scream.

"My baby. My baby. Save my baby girl. Save my baby. Someone."

"We are here at the tragic drowning of young Beatrice Bendetsen, age five, at Comoyga Pond. This is Nathalie Watson, Dynamic News, Channel Fourteen."

Nathalie smiled to the camera. The camera panned out to the pond. The little girl had come up again. The camera panned back to the mother. Then the girl. A producer behind the cameraman whispered:

"Stay on the girl going down. The mother's screaming is going to go on for half an hour. Plenty of footage there."

Nathalie Watson, her handsome, strong woman's face with fashionable swept hairdo, steamed over to the cameraman.

The producer was whispering furiously into some form of headset.

Nathalie ripped it off him.

"I will not do a voice-over. I have been doing voice-overs all day. I want live."

"Nathalie, precious, we love you but this is good footage," said the producer.

"There's always good footage. That's why I am doing voice-overs all day."

"It's the first drowning of the year, live," said the producer.

"Someone. Please. My girl," cried the mother, and then she looked at Remo, Remo who was turning away, Remo whose years of training served an organization that dared not be known to exist. Remo who, in the absolute best interests of his country, was a lone assassin, a man who didn't exist. And therefore could not be on a television camera, or photographed. He was a man whose fingerprints were no longer checked against files, because he was dead. Had been for well over a decade, the victim of a well-planned, carefully executed fake death. The man who didn't exist for the organization which didn't exist.

He had been trained to discipline his feelings. Thoughts, after all, were the real power of the human body, not the crude, weak muscles. Even his dreams at times were as controllable as fingertips. So he told himself he should not be bothered by this.

And then he saw the mother's eyes lock with his, and heard the word "please."

And all of it went. The years of it went. The training of it went. The analysis of the situation went. And Remo was moving, the legs following the force of the body, the absolute perfection of movement. Smooth, as though the legs were like feathers, and the air, not a barrier, but a moving part of a universe. He heard the pads of his shoes tap the thin ice like the soft pop of a cellophane cake wrapper. His feet did not pound the ice but moved with the mass of water beneath it, his thin body feeling the prickly cool of the still-chill Michigan spring. Pine trees, green and fragrant, rimmed the lake, and he could sense the weak rays of the sun on his body that floated as it moved, quick with the light feet. And then he was at the girl and with his left hand he scooped her up out of the water as though fielding a baseball and continued the open fifty yards to the rest of the ice on the other side of the lake.

It was that fifty yards that caused the cameraman to check his focus, the producer to let out a shriek, and even Nathalie Watson to stop complaining about her lack of camera time.

"Did you see that?" said the producer.

"Did I see what I saw?" said Nathalie.

"The guy ran on water."

"To hell with the drowning. We don't have it anyway unless the kid goes back in the water, which I don't think she will."

"I don't think she will either," said Nathalie. "That mother won't let her. I'll do a live with the man who runs on water."

"Okay," said the producer.

"What happened?" cried the mother, trying to brush the tears away to see her daughter better, her daughter now coming very quickly to her in the arms of that man who had gone out to save her. He was running with her along the lake shore. The mother hadn't seen what he had done. All she saw was that her daughter was going to live. The crowd behind her cheered.

Nathalie Watson moved through the crowd toward the mother. That was where the man who ran on water would be. With any luck, provided no one shot the President or something—and that could happen with bad luck—Nathalie Watson and her strong handsome woman's face were going to be on camera this evening not only Michigan north, but network national. She was heading toward thirty seconds of national exposure.

"What happened? What happened?" asked the mother.

"We're going to do an interview," said Nathalie.

"My baby," said the mother, and reached out her hands. Remo saw the hands, saw the pain and joy, and put the child back in her mother's arms.

And then he smiled. He was feeling very good again. Good as when he was seventeen in a New Jersey city drinking beer from a bottle, feeling very much grown-up the night before he was to enter the Marines. No. Better than that. Then he felt grown-up. Now he felt like a human being.

And there was the camera looking at him with the big glass eye that was not only going to spread his face all over the country but show those special things he could do, so that from now on everyone would be looking for him if he disappeared. As the television newswoman approved, pointing the microphone toward his face, he suddenly wondered if he should wave to the folks upstairs and say hello. He could see Smitty, the head of the organization, choking on air if he said hello. Maybe he should say:

"Hi, America. I'm Remo Williams, and I can do these wonderful things because I have had training no white man has ever had before—and damned few Koreans, too, maybe one every half-century or so. Maybe you've seen me before. I kill a lot. So here I am, Remo Williams, saying your government couldn't survive within the Constitution, so they have me break it high, wide, and handsome just so we can all survive from week to week, from one disaster to the next."

He thought of that as the mother was hugging the little girl, kissing the cheeks, laughing and crying and thanking Remo, and really only happy she had the child back. He thought it while Nathalie Watson was asking him if he realized what he did. He thought of it, and then he thought of lemon-faced Harold W. Smith, chief of the organization, choking at the televised proof that the secrecy so many had died for had been destroyed on an impulse. Whoopee. And Remo Williams began to laugh. And the laughter seized him.

"Sir, sir. Are you overjoyed? Is that why you are laughing?"

"No," laughed Remo.

"Why are you laughing?"

"Get the microphone out of my face," said Remo. There was moisture in his eyes.

The microphone came up closer to his lips.

"Get the microphone away from my face," said Remo. He was still laughing.

But Nathalie Watson, award-winning newscaster, was not going to be moved by something as insignificant as a personal request. Nathalie Watson, her good side toward the camera, moved the microphone a touch closer. Nathalie Watson saw the laughing man's hands. They seemed so slow. But somehow her hands were slower. Nathalie Watson was suddenly looking at the camera with a cord coming out of the center of her mouth. Something was lodged in her throat. It felt cold. It was metal. The microphone had a definite aluminum taste. She wondered what she looked like with a microphone cord coming out of her mouth. She looked at the camera and smiled. If the lunatic hadn't damaged her magnificent teeth, no harm would be done. She saw the laughing lunatic go up to the cameraman. He took the camera. The cameraman had been a linebacker at a Big Ten school. He had also gotten a degree in communications. This prepared him perfectly for carrying something heavy and pointing it. He did not take kindly to people grabbing his camera.

His playing weight had been 244 pounds of lean muscle. He had put on a bit more beef since then and now weighed 285. For the sake of beautiful Nathalie and his camera the lunatic was reaching for, the cameraman took a football-sized fist and pounded it down into his head. He was sure they would have to dig this guy out of the ground.

His fist felt quite funny as it struck. Was the guy's head metal? No. The truck was metal. The Channel 14 truck was all metal. It made a very loud sound. It made the sound because he was being thrown into it. It shivered and he collapsed.

Remo had the camera. He recognized it as the kind cameramen changed film with in one motion. One only had to slide it backward. It did not slide backward. Was it right-side-up? Remo slid the film magazine up. It did not slide up. Nor did it slide down or forward.

"It's a simple one-piece move," said the producer, who knew his film was going to be lost; now all he wanted was to save the camera.

"I did that," said Remo. This time he slid harder. He slid in all directions. A flaky gray cloud appeared in his hands, along with the film that smoldered with a bitter smell of burning tires. The camera had disintegrated from the friction. The film had been set on fire. He gave it back to the producer.

"Any idiot could have opened the damn thing," said the producer.

"Wrong idiot," said Remo pleasantly. One of these days he was going to have to learn how to work gadgets. He jumped up on the truck. There were about twenty people in the crowd.

"Look. I want a favor. I want you to say this never happened. I have personal reasons. Any reporters, including these people here, come to you and ask you about this, just say the girl fell in on the shore and her mother picked her out."

"You don't want credit for it?" called out a man from the crowd.

"I want you to say it never happened. Say the camera crew is on coke or something."

"Anything," cried the mother. The crowd closed around her, pointing at the crew.

"I saw them sniffing," said a woman, "didn't you?"

"Absolutely," said another.

One man in the crowd very quietly slipped away. He was a grain inspector for the government. He worked for the Department of Agriculture. He filed his reports on a computer terminal in his office in nearby Kalkaska, Michigan. About twenty years before, he had gotten a directive. The government, concerned with price fixing, wanted him to file reports on anything unusual. The request was general, and he wasn't sure what they wanted, but they did want him not to talk about it. He knew a couple of other grain inspectors in the Kalkaska office had gotten the same request, knew it because they mentioned how unusual it was. He said nothing because he was under the impression he wasn't supposed to talk about it. Shortly thereafter the other men were talking about how the program had been dropped. Just like the government, not knowing what it was doing.

But it wasn't dropped for him, and he realized he had just passed a weeding-out process. Early on, he used to phone in his reports to a special number. They were interested mainly in criminal activities. He never knew what good it did, but a couple of times, prosecutors nailed the people he had suspected, never knowing it might have been him who turned them onto it. One time a gangland figure notorious for eliminating witnesses turned up crushed like a grape in a room that only had an entrance through the twentieth floor. No one could figure out how they got a machine into that room to do that sort of damage. But the gang that had been preying on grain dealers disappeared with him.

When computers came in he was given a computer access number special to him. And he would punch in his code, punch in his information. There were two strange things about this. One, they wanted information on anything strange or different nowadays, not just Agriculture departmental business, and two, he never got an answer back except to confirm that it was sent. Each month he got a check from his department mailed to his home, sort of a bonus, nothing exceptional, but he knew he was the only one getting it.

Now as he drove through the Michigan countryside and its spring-sodden fields, he wondered about that. Wondered if he shouldn't pass up the incident at the pond. It wasn't illegal except possibly for the assault on the television people, and that the local police could handle if they ever could get a witness against the assaulter.

What the man had done was strange. Was it the sort of thing they would be interested in? He wondered again as he sat down to his terminal. He decided to make it brief. He was almost embarrassed to even report it.

"Saw man on pond run across water. Fifty yards. Did it to save a kid, then asked everyone to say they didn't see it. Destroyed television camera. Man seemed to have incredible force. Thought it might be of interest. Sorry if it isn't. It wowed me."

And then he punched in his code sign-off.

And for the first time in twenty years, he got an answer that was more than just an acknowledgment of a received message.

"Ran on water? How far?"

The Agriculture inspector's fingers suddenly felt numb. He punched the keys, hit several wrong characters, and had to repunch. Finally he got out the message.

"Fifty yards."

"Describe man."

"Thin, sort of. Dark hair. High cheekbones. Wore light jacket and loafers. Didn't seem to mind the cold."

"Did he have thick wrists?"

"Affirmative. They were thick."

"Did the television cameras get pictures of him?"

"Yes."

"Where is the film? Who has it? Is it scheduled for this evening? Answer if you know. Do not attempt to find out."

"Film burned up. Crew assaulted by man."

"Are they dead? Witnesses?"

"Not dead. Man got up on truck and told everyone to deny what they saw. Everyone willing because man saved little girl. I think no one minded television crew getting punched out."

"Punched out? Explain."

"Cameraman put up a fight."

"You said no one dead?"

"Correct."

"And film destroyed?"

"Correct."

The grain inspector saw the sign-off on the screen, and never heard from whoever was at the other end again. He wasn't even sure what continent the other terminal was on.

At the other terminal, Harold W. Smith looked out of the one-way windows of Folcroft Sanitarium on Long Island Sound and said one simple swear word. It had to do with human waste and began with an S. It referred to

the antics of Remo. Remo was now performing in front
of television cameras. He wondered whether he should
even use him anymore. Unfortunately, he had to.

Chiun, Master of Sinanju, glory of the name of
Sinanju, teacher of the youth from outside Sinanju
named Remo, prepared to enter into the history of
Sinanju the bald fact that Remo was white, possibly
without even a trace of natural yellow blood. He did this
in a hotel room with a scroll laid out before him.

The ugly gray light of the American city named
Dearborn, in the province of Michigan, filled the room
that was crowded with heavy American furniture. Big
wood chunks supported heavy brocaded pillows. Chiun
sat on his mat, an island of dignity surrounded by the
accoutrements of the new world. The television set, the
one magnificent thing in the cesspool of this culture, was
off.

His topaz writing kimono was still. His delicate hand
with the graceful long fingernails carefully dipped the
quill into the dark inkbowl. He had been leading up to
this moment for years, first hinting that Remo, who
would be the next Master of Sinanju, had come from
outside the village of Sinanju, then outside Korea itself,
then even to the point of referring to where Remo was
born as being beyond the Orient. Now he would say it:
Chiun had given Sinanju, the sun source of all the
martial arts, to a white. The House of Sinanju would one
day be inherited by a white. He felt the ages of these
greatest assassins looking down on him. The great
Wang, who had done so much to elevate the Masters of
Sinanju, taking them from positions of servitude in the
courts of the Chinese dynasties to legendary status.
Master Toksa, who had taught the lesson to the

pharaohs. The Lesser Wang. And there was little Gi, who had determined that the reason Sinanju had unlocked the full power of the human animal was that it was the most perfect product of the most perfect race. Little Gi was never a great assassin, but he was the most loved historian of all the Masters of Sinanju. Little Gi looked down on Chiun the hardest. It was little Gi who once believed that power to be a great assassin was in the color of the skin.

It was Gi who had convinced Kublai Khan to rise above Mongol barbarism, to stop doing their own sloppy assassinations and to let professionals like Sinanju serve a great court.

To this Kublai Khan agreed, and asked that little Gi teach his son such body control. Now, understanding the minds of emperors, Gi knew he would not refuse. Nor could he fail. But the boy was clumsy, stupid, and unable to follow directions despite an agreeable nature. He had the intelligence and natural agility of a clod of mud. It had been a triumph to get the boy across a room on both feet.

"Great emperor," Gi told his father, the Khan, Kublai, "your seed shows an infinite ability to excel, to excel to such an extent that he must command assassins, not dirty his hand like some horseman."

Now Kublai's father was Tamerlane, son of Genghis, the Khan. And they were Mongols, horse Mongols, riding Mongols, killing Mongols, who took great pride in their horses and swords and bloody massacres. Their method of rule was simple terror, and they left the greatest of the cities of the world, like Baghdad, in cinders. They were as fit to rule as a child throwing a tantrum for a toy. Tamerlane's Mongols, being barbarians, of course had no need of an assassin. They did not understand that if one had an assassin one could kill few instead of many, one could rule cities instead of pillage them.

Kublai understood, but still liked to pride himself on being Mongol, a horse Mongol. So when Gi referred to the Khan's son as more than a horse rider, Kublai became furious. He said his son was Mongol, as Mongol as Genghis and Tamerlane, as Mongol as the plains from which they came. Now this was said in the imperial city of Cathay amid the splendor of silks and cushions and pools of perfume, lily pads of gold flake and women of such beauty as to turn the eyes of statues.

"No, great emperor. You are greater than your father, and your son, greater than you. And his son shall be greater still, because you are the ones meant to rule the world. Men ride horses from saddles, but they ride men from thrones. Now which I ask you is greater?"

And Kublai Khan had to agree ruling men was greater than ruling horses. And little Gi then pointed out that when a royal attempted to do the work of an assassin, a royal was not as great as he could be by ruling assassins.

For if the Khan gave up the idea of his son learning Sinanju, then the son would be yet greater still because he would rule assassins. Little Gi not only got rid of a hopeless dolt, for Mongols never could move like Koreans, but he also earned more tributes from the great Khan at the same time.

Later generations, bereft of suitable candidates in the village and the peninsula, would attempt to teach a Thai, even an arrogant Japanese, who later took the meager scraps of Sinanju and turned them into Ninja. But none but Sinanju were successful, in thousands of years.

Now the most un-Sinanju person in imagination, an American white of dubious parentage, had become in all manner and thought, but for regressive white habits, a full Master of Sinanju. And Chiun had to explain how, and most importantly why, he had chosen such an unlikely student.

The subject had been introduced in previous chapters of Chiun's histories by implication: the Master hinted strongly that America was a form of an extension of the Korean peninsula, stressing that the Indians who crossed over from the Bering Strait were Oriental in origin. In a few thousand years only a handful of scholars would know the difference anyhow. And besides, there was always that good Korean girl who would take Remo's seed and begin the breeding-out process. A simple sixteen generations should purify the line adequately.

And then no one would know. But Chiun had come to the part where the parentage of Remo had to be written and he certainly could not enter Remo's origin into the history of Sinanju as "not exactly in the center of the village of Sinanju proper," or even "the far suburbs." America was America was America and not, in truth, an extension of the Korean peninsula. Future masters would have maps, and Chiun did not wish to be remembered as one who told untruths. He had been working on Remo many years now, first to get him to write a history, which he wouldn't, and second to refer to Chiun as the "Great Chiun." A great Master was established by future generations.

So Chiun now was poised with ink-heavy quill over the lambskin parchment, the Korean symbol for white in his mind, ready to see it on the scroll.

And then Remo entered the hotel room. Chiun knew it was Remo because the door did not open with grinding of metal on hinge but rather balanced and silent, resting naturally on the handle and the hinge. Also, there was not the cold thump of weight falling on the balls of the feet, or the odor of meat-laden breathing used by those who breathed the way they were born.

The person entered the room with the grace of the wind, and the only other who would do that now was Remo.

Chiun immediately put the quill back in the well and asked if Remo would like to begin training in recording events of history.

"Anything you wish to say," said Chiun, his white wisps of hair trembling with joy.

"Why are you happy to see me, little father?" said Remo.

"I am always happy to see you."

"Not that happy. What's wrong?"

"Nothing is wrong."

"Is that the same scroll I left you with this morning?" said Remo. He glanced at the letter symbols of grace and power, an elegant writing. Not only hadn't Chiun advanced much since the morning, he was stuck on that same word.

Remo turned on the television to Channel 14 Dynamic News. There was a lot of active-authoritative music, then a graphic that faded into a shot of people sitting around talking. Then the people sitting around talking were shown talking to people who were not employed by Channel 14. These were politicians. There was a fire. Channel 14 people talked to firemen. At every change there was the music. Armies could have marched to that music. Channel 14 could have run excerpts from the fall of Berlin to that music.

Nathalie Watson was not there. An anchorman talked about it. He talked about the horror of assaults on newsmen attempting to keep America free. He talked about a reporter's word being the most trustworthy element in any story.

"Boldly and proudly we at Channel Fourteen Dynamic News declare forthrightly that concerning the situation in the lake district, we will not comment. And we might add that at Channel Fourteen, we lead the fight against drugs. Ms. Watson will return just as soon as surgeons extricate a Channel Fourteen Dynamic News microphone from her esophagus."

The martial music went on again.

Safe, thought Remo. He had gotten away with it. And he was feeling good. He looked to Chiun. Chiun was smiling. He was not even angry that Remo had turned to something else, not focusing immediately on what Chiun had brought up.

"What is it?" said Remo.

"Nothing," said Chiun. "I am looking for just the right word for the history that you will take over someday. I thought perhaps you might help with the word."

"What word do you want me to help with?"

"Perhaps you can write something about your not telling me your parentage and that your movements have always been Sinanju upon being shown them so well by, say, the Great Chiun."

"Do you want me to call you Great?"

"Do you want to call me Great?" said Chiun. "If you want to, that is your right. As you become a full Master of Sinanju when I am no longer here, I know you will want to remember me with accuracy and honor."

"I don't know what Great is. I don't know any other Masters."

"If you read the histories you would know what Great is."

"I read them. They're distorted. Ivan the Terrible is

Ivan the Good because he paid on time. The whole
world revolves around what is good for Sinanju and
what is not. The histories are mostly nonsense. I know
that now. I'm not a trainee anymore."

"Sacrilege," said Chiun. The head rose in righteous
umbrage.

"Truth," said Remo. "They're fairy tales."

"The histories of Sinanju are what make you and me
what we are. They are our past, and our future. They are
our strength."

"Then if they are so accurate, why do you want me to
lie?"

"Put in your own words, then, what you call truth."

Remo glanced at the scroll.

"White. The word you want is 'white.' Do you want
me to write it? My characters are not as fine as yours but
I will write it. I'm white."

"That's so crude," said Chiun. "Perhaps you can say it
with grace. Say, perhaps, that strangers would get a
white impression from you but because of the way you
have been taught to move and excel you are Korean in
essence."

"I'm white," said Remo. "The character sign is
'white.' You know, the pale lake surrounded by the
bleaching sticks. Do you want me to write it?"

"I wanted help," said Chiun, "and I got you." He
cleaned the quill in pure vinegar and wax-sealed the
special ink blended to last millennia for future Masters
of Sinanju. He would write no more until the foulness of
this betrayal left his spirits. "I can write no more for
years."

"You didn't want to say I was white," said Remo.

"Your problem is you have never worked for a real
emperor."

The phone rang and a computer was talking to him.

Remo knew who was behind it. But Smitty, Harold W. Smith, head of the organization, hadn't reached out for him like that in years, partly because Remo had difficulty in working the codes, but also because assignments often required questions and answers. This was an old and cumbersome routine. Remo got the first code right in answering the computer. It was to hit the number one on the touch-tone phone continuously until what at first appeared to be a sales pitch from a computer turned into a responding voice, still not Smith. It instructed him to make sure no one was following him and to proceed to a phone booth in nearby Lansing, Michigan. The code to punch in that phone booth was a continuous two.

It was downtown Lansing and Remo arrived there at night. And after he put in his quarter and punched two continuously, he finally got Smith's voice.

"What's wrong? What's up?"

"You went running across water in front of a television camera today."

"Yes. I did," said Remo.

"Therefore, you threatened to compromise the entire organization."

"I saved a little girl."

"And we're trying to save a country, Remo."

"Right then," said Remo, "I felt the little girl was more important. And do you want to know something? I still do."

"Are you in the mood to help your civilization?"

"What do you mean by that?"

"Uranium is being stolen continuously from factories and we cannot stop it. So far, enough uranium to make fourteen atomic bombs is missing. We don't know how they are doing it. All other intelligence agencies are helpless. We're down to you, Remo."

"I never thought I was down, Smitty," said Remo.

"We are a last resort," said Smith. "We have to get you into one of the factories."

"Smitty . . ."

"Yeah."

"If I had it to do over again, I would still save that girl."

"I know," said Smith.

"You know me."

"That's why I said it. Watch yourself."

"What's to watch? I'm always okay."

Across the safe line Remo heard Harold W. Smith clear his throat. Remo did not mention that he would have loved to see Smith's face if the pictures did appear on network TV. Then he would have loved it. Now he felt sort of bad. He felt he had betrayed a trust, a trust to this man and a trust given by a nation.

"I'll watch it," said Remo finally. He said it with anger. He hung up by embedding the plastic receiver into the phone and shattering the booth door as he walked out through it in a shower of wire-reinforced glass.

From across the street it looked as though the telephone booth had exploded the man out of it. It looked that way to the policeman who saw the suspicious-looking stranger who did it. But the longer the cop watched the stranger, the more unsuspicious he became, especially when, just as an angry boy might kick a can, he took a car door off and skimmed it down the street. The policeman then remembered a sudden parking problem in the opposite direction and ran there to write the tickets.

3

Harrison Caldwell knew gold. Anyone who trusted anything else was a fool. In times of crisis, people bought gold with their paper and their land and their possessions. And when the price of gold went up, then Caldwell and Sons, est. 1402, goldbrokers to the world, bullionists supreme, would sell gold. It was a nervous time. The paper was called money, but it was based only on people's faith. Eventually all paper came to be worth its weight in wood pulp. When that happened slowly, it was called inflation. When it happened quickly, it was called a collapse.

Selling gold for paper always made the Caldwells nervous. They only held the paper as long as the price of gold was high, waiting for the gold to moderate. That was the kind of patience that brought a man two things he could not have too much of. One was gold; the other was heads on the wall.

"He who hangs his enemy's head on his palace wall may rest his easily for another night."

The Caldwells had operated in the Americas since the sixteenth century, and in New York City since 1701, occupying the same family-owned land near the port for over two hundred years. Later that little street just off Wall Street in the commercial district would be worth millions. But the Caldwells knew that land, too, had flaws. Land was only worth what people said it was worth; therefore, it was nearly as weak an investment as paper. And as for ownership, armies decided who owned what land. Nobody ever stopped an invasion with a silly little piece of paper called a deed.

Only gold was of value forever. When the Caldwells had lost everything once in Europe, they escaped with only the knowledge that gold endured, and tales of a great stone that someday one of their descendants might discover again. "Gold," they had told every firstborn son, "begins and ends every hope of man. With enough gold, anything you want will be yours."

And now Harrison Caldwell was going to own more of it than anyone. The pictures of the stone and the translation from the old alchemist's symbols were safely locked in the Caldwell depository in a major New York City bank. The dead, of course, were dead, and therefore completely safe. While their heads didn't hang on palace walls to give warning, they would keep their silence more certainly than a promise from a saint's lip.

It was Harrison Caldwell's own personal wonderful day. He left the sedate offices of Caldwell and Sons, bullionists, happy, receiving awestruck recognition from the line of secretaries leading to the front door.

"Mr. Caldwell," each would say, and Harrison Caldwell would nod. Sometimes he would see a flower on a desk out of place, or a fingernail bitten. Though he would not say anything to the offending secretary herself, he would mention it later to an assistant. The secretary would then be reminded to mend her ways.

The wages were relatively low, the demands precise and unmovable, and despite what every labor-relations counselor would call a throwback to the Stone Age, Caldwell and Sons had a turnover rate of virtually nil, while those corporations with "enrichment programs" and "employee feedback forums" and psychological tests had the pass-through rate of a subway turnstile.

Caldwell and Sons did not have employee feedback forums and the employees knew why: they were not the chums of the Caldwells, nor were they partners in an enterprise. They were employees. In that respect they would be paid on time, given clear work, not overworked one day or idled the next. They could advance in pay as their skills advanced. There was something about working at Caldwell and Sons that was reassuring.

"I don't know what it is. You just always know where you stand. It's weird. You just have to be in Mr. Caldwell's presence to know where you are in relation to where he is." This, invariably, came from each new employee.

And where they stood, where everyone who worked for Harrison Caldwell stood, was beneath him. And the great secret he knew was that most of the people in the world liked that. The Caldwells knew how to rule.

So, on this day as he left, all the secretaries were surprised to see him lay his hand on an assistant's shoulder. They would have been more surprised if they heard what he had said. But all they heard was the assistant's rather loud reply:

"Are you sure? Are you sure, Mr. Caldwell?"

Then they saw Harrison Caldwell nod ever so slightly. If they didn't know him, they would not even have known it was a nod. But that was the Caldwell nod. Three times the assistant asked the same question, and three times there was the nod.

After the assistant bowed his good-bye, he stumbled

back to his own office. There he sat down, cleared his
desk, and set the telephone directly in the middle of it.
Next, he ordered that no phone calls were to be put
through to him unless they came from Mr. Caldwell
himself.

Then he waited, staring at the telephone, as the
perspiration formed on his forehead. For what Mr.
Harrison Caldwell, the most conservative broker in a
conservative business, had just told him was that when
he phoned, Caldwell and Sons was to immediately sell
twice as much gold as they had, or possibly hoped to
have. And this plan was to be carried out in seven
languages in seven countries.

Harrison Caldwell left his office humming and entered
his chauffeur-driven limousine, promptly giving his
driver an address in a part of Harlem few whites ever
entered.

For Harrison Caldwell, Harlem was one of the safer
places in the world, because he understood the black
ghetto. It was not unsafe; it was just unsafe for people
without guns or unwilling to use them. During the riots
of the sixties when stores and buildings went up in
flames, several buildings were left unscathed. And these
were not black-owned places, but those owned by the
mob.

While commentators throughout the country placed
the blame of the riots on deprivation, racial injustice,
and all manner of social ills, Harrison Caldwell and the
Mafia knew a far more basic reason for the destruction.
A very human reason. The rioters knew they were not
going to be shot, except when they entered mob-run
stores.

These remained as peaceful as Fifth Avenue.

And so would Harrison Caldwell's warehouse. It was a
bastion neither riot nor arson nor anarchy could

penetrate. Nevertheless, Harrison Caldwell took his precautions one step further when he ordered that everything being brought into his warehouse be delivered in giant drums, drums so large that only a crane could move them. Since nothing could be snatched and run with, even the random street crime that plagued the neighborhood would not affect him.

He entered his warehouse at noon and went to a glass-enclosed booth high above the floor. Beneath him were bubbling vats of molten lead and sulfur. He looked at his watch. The trucks should be arriving soon, he thought. Time for a final check. As he requested, each door was guarded by a man with a shotgun. These were rented by Caldwell from a local gangster. Outside there was the growl of heavy trucks, coughing their way to a halt. The guards checked their weapons and glanced toward the booth. Caldwell nodded for them to let the trucks in. The heavy metal doors to his warehouse creaked open and three trucks lumbered into the building and parked near giant hoists. Immediately the hoists dropped metal claws into the backs of the trucks and picked up, drum by drum, the yellow barrels marked with the black crosses that signified nuclear danger, careful to set them right, without spilling. What pleased Harrison Caldwell most was not how perfectly the hoists set each drum in its preordained position, nor how the warehouse staff functioned as one, but the very fact that the trucks had arrived on time. For it had taken him months to gather this material, to put together all of the small and large quantities that made up the contents of three trucks. Harrison Caldwell was watching months and a dozen little acts all coming together at the specified time to join the bubbling vats of lead and sulfur in proper proportions. He was watching himself become the richest man who ever lived. As he saw the trucks unload tons of the one material the ancient alchemists lacked, he felt his ancestors were applauding in their royal way. They were right—it was possible to make gold from lead and mercury. All they had to do was add the ingredients symbolized on the stone, an element incredibly rare in their age, but plentiful today. All they needed was uranium, and all the Caldwells could have forged their futures on the philosopher's stone. After all, the secret to how he knew the stone and its one ancient flaw was the very history of his family.

As was the adage: "He who holds gold holds the soul of the world." Not that Harrison Caldwell wanted the soul of the world. He only dealt in what was of value.

He himself directed the emptying of the drums into a vat, watching it fill up to a mark he had made on its side. Harrison Caldwell had taken the formula inscribed on that stone now beneath the Atlantic and multiplied it by twenty thousand. The proportions were immense. What had been a mouse-hair's pinch in alchemic terms was now exactly five tons of uranium. The lead was seventy-three-point-eight, by weight. The sulfur would only act as a catalyst.

Three chrome-plated steel funnels twenty yards long all led to a white-faced wall and a single funnel. No one in the mixing room would see what came out the back.

Harrison Caldwell returned to his office and entered the only passage to the back room, a small man-size circular stairway. There were no doors to that room. He flicked on a light. A vast cavern lit up. The floor beneath him, one hundred yards by one hundred yards, looked like a checkerboard run amok. And on that floor, thousands of oblong molds were laid out at a precise angle, so that those closest to the funnel were slightly higher than those farther away.

A lesser man might have sweat or yelled. But Harrison Caldwell simply threw a switch. On the other side of the wall the vats tilted. Molten lead flowed alongside burning sulfur and mercury; then came a stream of the uranium, called so quaintly by the alchemists, "owl's teeth." Uranium, of course, had nothing to do with teeth at all. Professor Cryx had given his life to explain that to Harrison Caldwell.

The hot metals made a cracking sound as they joined at the wall and went on through, gray and pink and red. But when they came out mixed, they had turned magnificent yellow, with a light white coat of dross skimming the top. What was now pouring out into the thousands of molds was gold. Twenty-four karat gold. Exactly seventy-eight-point-three tons of it, forming at his feet a floor full of gold bars in a world where that simple, soft metal sold for $365 an ounce.

In the offices of Caldwell and Sons, the assistant, on his eighth tranquilizer of the hour, got a phone call. He remained as calm as if Mr. Caldwell were ordering biscuits.

"Sell," came the aristocratic voice of Harrison Caldwell.

In Bayonne, New Jersey, the three drivers who had made a routine delivery of uranium for the federal agency controlling it were pulled over by a car with a blinking bubble on top.

A man with a badge hopped out of the car and asked the three drivers their names. Then he asked where they were taking the trucks.

"Back to the garage," said a driver. The man with the badge wrote down the address of the garage.

"Have you been carrying uranium?"

"Sure. What do you think those trucks are lined with lead for? Stops radiation. What do you think we wear radiation cards for? Why the questions?"

"We've had a problem. Large quantities of uranium have been missing from plants across the country. We're checking all transport."

"We got our bills of lading."

"I'd like to see them," said the man, putting his badge away. "All of them."

The three drivers returned to their trucks. It was a cold gray sort of day, and they had been looking forward to parking them for good and getting a beer. The trucks idled their big diesels on Kennedy Boulevard, a well-traveled road. Several people stopped to watch.

The man with the badge looked at the bills of lading and mentioned that nowhere did they show a stop in Harlem.

"Oh, that. Yeah. I'll give you the address."

"Wasn't that supposed to be secret?" said the man with the badge. "Weren't you supposed to keep your mouths shut, under any circumstances?"

"You're with the government, ain't ya?"

The man with the badge smiled. He beckoned them closer, returning their bills of lading. Each bill had an envelope with it. Each envelope had a note. It told them to look up. They were being robbed.

The big barrel of the .357 Magnum, a cannon of a pistol, told them to believe what they read. One of them began trembling. He couldn't get off his watch.

"Just a couple of wallets will be fine," he said. They didn't ask why he wanted only two. They thought of themselves as lucky. And this thought lasted less than three seconds because the big barrel of the pistol made flashes. They saw the flashes before they heard the sounds. Sound traveled at six hundred miles per hour.

The .357 Magnum slugs traveled faster, right through their skulls, taking off the tops of their heads, spilling their brains out onto Kennedy Boulevard.

A passing car slowed down, the man jumped in, and was driven to the Bayonne Bridge, a high-rising arch that reached across to Staten Island. At its apex he tossed out his badge. Everything had worked perfectly, just as he had been told. And just as he had been told, he was given his payoff near a public golf course on Staten Island. And this is where the plan changed. He did not get an envelope with thirty thousand dollars in it. He was given, instead, a brand-new shovel and allowed to dig his own grave.

When he finished, he was told not to bother to climb out.

"Hey, buddy. If they are going to pay me off like this," said the man in the open grave, "what do you think they are going to do to you?"

"Give me the shovel," said the man standing above the grave. He had light blond hair and delicate features, and a soft gentle mouth. When he got the shovel he appeared to be offering it back into the grave for help to climb out. But with a tender little giggle, he brought the blade of the shovel around, bludgeoning the larynx of the man already in the grave. Then, with a pleasant little laugh, he covered the body with the fresh earth just before a nearby golfer sliced into the area. The white ball landed in the soft fresh mound of the grave. The golfer walked over, and seeing it half-buried, cursed his luck.

"I mean it is like playing out of sand, right? I mean, is this ground under repair? Because if this is ground under repair, I get a free lift."

"No. You don't get a free lift. It's not ground under repair."

"You're cruel, you know," said the golfer. "You could have said it was ground under repair."

The next day, every Dynamic News station in every Dynamic News locale reported the simple murder for robbery of three drivers for a nuclear plant, and a denial by a government agency that any uranium was missing.

"While we deeply regret the murder/robbery of three of our drivers, we find no reason for a nuclear alarm."

This from a government spokesperson.

"But the trucks were empty, weren't they?" This from a newsperson.

"They were empty trucks en route to the main garage in Pennsylvania."

"But were they empty when they started out?"

"Yes."

"Then why were they being driven?"

"To return them to the main garage in Pennsylvania."

And the spokesperson assured the press, assured the television cameras and the world, there was nothing to worry about at this time. Everything was under control.

In his office just off Wall Street, Harrison Caldwell watched the bullion market take five tons without a quiver. Then he made arrangements to sell twice as much. He had just figured out a way to perfect the gathering of uranium. When you had an infinite amount of money, nothing was impossible.

4

It was a disgrace. It was an insult and humiliation almost too much to bear. But Chiun would bear it. He would bear it with dignity and in silence. Though he certainly could have borne it longer if Remo hadn't ignored the silence. For silence ignored was the most insulting if not useless of things. One might as well be a silent rock. And Chiun, Master of Sinanju, was not a rock. When he wasn't talking to someone, the victim had better know it.

"I am silent," he said, with a haughty rise of his gray-and-gold kimono of the day.

"I heard," said Remo. He showed his and Chiun's identification at the large cyclone fence surrounding the McKeesport, Pennsylvania, special nuclear facility. This was only one of the plants where uranium had been stolen. But three trucks destined for this plant did not arrive because their drivers had been robbed and murdered in a small New Jersey city. It sounded suspicious. Three dead men for two wallets containing less than a hundred and fifty dollars. Of course nowadays that kind of thing was as common as a rock in the forest. But there was just no place else to start. All

the investigative agencies had come up with nothing.
Remo wasn't sure what he could come up with, but he
supposed Smitty had wanted a new fresh look.

"I am still silent," said Chiun.

"All right," said Remo. "I am sorry. What are you
silent about?"

Chiun turned his head away. When one was silent,
one certainly wasn't going to discuss it.

The identification specified that Remo and Chiun
were nuclear engineers and they were going to rate the
plant, and any plant for that matter, for efficiency. This
enabled them to ask any question, no matter how stupid.

Remo asked where the uranium was stored prior to
shipment and was told it was not. All uranium had a
destination before it was made hot, as they called it.

Chiun touched Remo's arm.

"I know, little father, you're silent. Look at this stuff.
It's interesting. All those pipes."

"Excuse me, sir," said a guard. "Is there something in
particular you're looking at?"

"I'm just amazed by modern technology."

"That's not quite modern, sir. That's a men's room."

"Right," said Remo.

"May I see your identification?"

The guard looked at the two glossy cards that showed
vague likenesses of Remo and Chiun as nuclear
engineers. The pictures could never quite identify them,
but when showed, neither could they be used to prove
they weren't who they said they were. The pictures had
all the clarity and quality of normal passport photos.

"Would you come with me, please, sir."

"No," said Remo. He took back the card, even with
the guard's hands following after it.

"You're supposed to come with me. You can get hurt.
You don't even have a radiation badge."

"I don't need one. I can feel it."

"Nobody can feel radiation."

"You could if you listened to your body," said Remo. Chiun turned his head away in disgust. It was Remo's nature to attempt to explain things to any sort of fool. One could even smell the odors of cow meat coming from the breath of the guard, and Remo was talking to him about listening to his body. The absurdity of it all. Suddenly Chiun had so many reasons to keep silent that he gave up.

"Fool," he said to Remo. "We have been reduced to speaking to guards, to little spear carriers, to people not even policemen with little square badges and no honor. Why do you waste your time talking to eaters of dead cows?"

"I told him we didn't need radiation badges."

"We need brains is what we need. I have trained you as an assassin and now you wander around looking for thieves. We do not look for thieves. Policemen look for thieves. Your problem is you have never worked for a real emperor."

"Our country has a problem. This stuff can be used to make bombs that can destroy cities. Can you imagine entire cities being incinerated?"

"Today. Of course. Everything loses its grandeur. They destroy cities without even sack or pillage. And who recognizes the assassin today? A good, not even great assassin would save millions of lives."

"Do you know how many people were killed at Hiroshima?"

"Not as many as the Japanese killed by hand in the rape of Nanking. The weapons are not the problems. Armies are the problems, armies not even made of soldiers anymore, but citizens. Everyone is his own assassin. What a shame this age has become. And you

have taken the training I have given you and joined
the general degradation of your kind," said Chiun,
and began the litany of how he should have known
when first he tried to teach a white that the white
would revert to white ways. This he said following
Remo throughout the nuclear plant, in the cadence of
the Korean spoken most heavily in the northwest of
that peninsula called by the Masters of Sinanju "the
glory cove." For his big finish he stressed again that
they would not be so degraded if Remo worked for a real
emperor, not Smith the lunatic.

As they toured the plant, the director of security, a
woman in a smart suit with smart eyeglasses and a very
smart manner about her walk, watched the two. Remo
ignored her.

"Oh, gracious lady, I see that you, too, suffer."

"My name is Consuelo Bonner," said the woman. "I
am director of security, and I am not a lady, I am a
woman. And what are you two doing here?"

"Shh," said Remo. "I'm thinking."

"He does not realize your beauty, madam," said
Chiun.

"Would you shush a man?" said Consuelo Bonner.
She was twenty-eight years old, and could have been a
model with her flashing blue eyes and glorious pale skin
with raven hair, but chose instead to be in a business
where men would not order her around.

"No. I wouldn't shush a man in your job. I would put
him through a wall," said Remo.

"You don't sound like a nuclear engineer," said
Consuelo Bonner. "What is the fission rate of a neutron
imbalance subjected to hyperbombardment of laser-
intensified electron streams?"

"A good question," said Remo.

"Answer it or you're under arrest."

"Seven," said Remo.

"What?" said Consuelo Bonner. The answer was a formula.

"Twelve," said Remo.

"Ridiculous," said Consuelo Bonner.

"A hundred and twelve," said Remo. He turned away from the woman and continued on down the corridors of the plant, putting the problem into perspective. If the nuclear waste were stolen, he reasoned, the thefts could not have been committed by people without protection from radiation. It really couldn't even have been heisted by people who didn't know how to move the uranium; not that much uranium, and not that consistently. Therefore it probably was someone working within the system itself, someone who normally would have access to the fuel.

The woman was still following him. She had a walkie-talkie and was calling for assistance. Chiun smiled at the woman, telling Remo he had to learn how to handle women. One did not bruise them; one showered them with petals of distraction. He turned toward the woman, intent upon providing a gracious example.

"The delicacy of your hands on that instrument belies its purpose," said Chiun. "You are a thousand mornings of joy and delight."

"I am every bit as good as a man. I can do anything you can do, let me tell you that. Especially you, buddy, who won't even listen to me," she said.

"What?" said Remo.

"I said I am going to arrest you. I can do anything a man can do."

"Piss out a window," said Remo, still looking for the storage room. He could recognize lavatories now. They had the big atomic-looking pipes going to them. The reactor had the small-bathroom kind of piping. He would have this facility down pat in minutes.

Consuelo Bonner shrewdly waited until she had overwhelming force Eight guards. Four for each.

"This is your last chance. This is a federally protected area. You are here under suspicious circumstances, and I must ask you to come with me. If you refuse, I must place you under arrest."

"Piss out a window," said Remo.

"How crude to such an elegant lady," said Chiun.

"Arrest them," said Consuelo.

The guards split into two teams of four, and as they were trained, each closed in a perfect diamond pattern designed to make the perpetrator helpless. Except that they closed in on themselves. Consuelo Bonner blinked. She had these men trained at the best police schools. She had seen them work out herself. She had seen one break a board with his head. They all had martial-arts experience and now they were bumping heads like babies in a playpen.

"Move it," she snapped. "Use clubs. Anything. Guns. They are just walking away from you."

The guards abandoned their patterns and with a yell all eight, like a vengeful herd, fell on the two walking down the hall as casually as though strolling through a meadow.

Two of the eight were able to stand at the end of the skirmish and a third said he felt nothing. The invading pair kept on walking. Consuelo Bonner took off her eyeglasses. She would approach the elder of the pair. He, at least, was a gentleman.

"I guess I didn't understand you. I just want to keep my plant safe."

"From uranium being stolen," said Remo.

"You can't prove that. This plant is as safe as if a man ran it," said Consuelo.

"That's what I'm saying. It's a mess."

"You don't think men are better?" said Consuelo.

"We think we are forever denied having children," said Chiun. "So we make do with our meager awesome powers."

Consuelo Bonner followed them down the hall.

"If you are not engineers, who are you?"

"People who may have the same interest as you," said Remo.

"To exalt your beauty," said Chiun.

In Korean, Remo told Chiun that this woman didn't seem receptive to that sort of flattery. Chiun answered, also in Korean, that Remo was acting too white. What would it hurt to make a poor life a little less dreary with a kind word? Chiun knew how to live without gratitude. He had learned that teaching Remo. But why should an innocent woman suffer?

"For the last time, I'm not going to write that I am not white. I'm not going to imply that I lied to you, or that something in your teaching made me Korean. I am white. I have always been white. I will always be white. And when I write the history of Sinanju . . ."

Chiun raised a hand. "You will write that we are nothing but hired guards and the great House of Sinanju, assassins to the world, have been reduced to servants."

"We're saving a country."

"What has the country ever done for you? What has the country ever taught you? What is your country? There are thousands of countries and there will be thousands more. But Sinanju is here tomorrow and tomorrow and tomorrow . . . if you don't fail us."

"I am not marrying some fat ugly girl from Sinanju, either," said Remo.

Now all of this was said in Korean, like machine-gun fire. Consuelo Bonner did not understand a word. But she knew it was an argument. She also judged without any difficulty that these two had as much to do with nuclear science as a pinball machine. She also knew that eight guards were useless against them, and that they were probably able to take on many more than that.

But Consuelo Bonner had not gotten to be chief of security at a nuclear plant by taking leaps at suspicions. Women, she knew, were judged more harshly than men. She was all but certain these two men might be just what she needed to get back her fuel, to get her the credit for getting back the fuel, and for taking one more small step for her gender. To say nothing of the large one for her pocketbook.

"I know who you are," she said. "You're not engineers. You're from one of the zillion federal agencies trying to track down the fuel. We've had them all, I think. Hasn't been made public because they don't want to panic anyone about enough fuel for dozens of bombs floating around. But I can help you find the trail of the fuel."

Remo stopped. He looked to Chiun. Chiun looked away, still angered.

"Okay," said Remo. "But tell me. What was the answer to your first question that gave you the hint I might not be a nuclear engineer? Was it seven? I had a hunch it was seven."

"It's a formula. What do you want to know for?"

"In case someone asks me again," said Remo.

Chiun turned slowly to the young white woman encouraging Remo to be a finder of lost things. He looked at her smooth white skin and sharp Western suit.

Harlot, he thought.

"A penny for your thoughts," said Consuelo.

Chiun smiled, and tugged Remo away from the woman.

Harrison Caldwell felt his stomach tighten. His palms moistened and his lips went dry, and once again he felt fear. But he could not show fear. To this man he could show neither fear nor dishonesty. He was the one man you did not lie to. Nor did you use him carelessly. Shrewdly, Harrison Caldwell had kept him in reserve for only the right times, only the right missions. For as the family had said:

"Money, without a sword, is a gift for whoever has one." Harrison Caldwell had not used him for the professor who translated the stone, nor of course for the divers. Harrison Caldwell only used Francisco Braun when it was absolutely necessary. He was the last step.

Harrison Caldwell was one of the few men who knew how to use an assassin. One did not squander him for one's ego, nor belittle him as a hireling.

"Treat your sword as your daughter, and you will die of old age." And by that, it was meant that one did not go to one's sword willy-nilly for every niggling problem, or even every killing. Harrison Caldwell was not a squeamish man, but Francisco Braun could turn a stomach of iron to jelly. Sometimes, since he had found him, Harrison Caldwell wondered if Francisco knew just how terrifying he was. He had found Francisco on the Barcelona waterfront. Knowing he would need a sword to attain great wealth, he had gone to the worst section of Barcelona and asked for the name of the most ferocious killer.

Popular opinion led him to the man who ran a heroin-refining operation, known to kill his competition by breaking in their ribs and puncturing their lungs, letting them die by drowning, so to speak, in the very dry streets of Barcelona. Harrison Caldwell offered one hundred thousand dollars to the man who killed him. Caldwell's explanation was that he was seeking revenge for a relative who had died through drugs. When one offered a hundred thousand dollars, one did not need a very good explanation.

Though Barcelona's streets became littered with still men and caved chests, still they came from around the world. Whites, blacks, yellows came and died in the streets of Barcelona. Harrison Caldwell himself read about these things safely from a Paris hotel suite.

Then, after three weeks of carnage, the drug dealer was found in bed with his stomach ever so neatly fricasseed, and a gentle blond man came to the hotel asking for his money. At first, Caldwell could not believe such a pretty young man could have been the killer. The concierge downstairs thought him a male prostitute, a homosexual prostitute, such was the gentleness of the features. But something about the man's ease told Harrison Caldwell this pretty young man had done the job.

"I promised a hundred thousand dollars," Caldwell said. "I lied. It is four hundred thousand dollars. One hundred thousand dollars now, and three hundred thousand dollars to come in a short time: in gold."

"Why three hundred thousand dollars?" said the young man.

"Because you will never work for anyone else again. You are my sword."

He waited while the young man thought this over. Caldwell knew that someone who could kill with this ferocity just might kill him for daring to say such a thing. But if he said yes, Harrison Caldwell would have his sword.

"Yes," said Francisco Braun. As soon as Harrison Caldwell discovered that uranium was the missing element, his sword had work. And precise work too. He could take out a man's eyes as easily as he could help someone "in his sleep." Francisco Braun could kill anywhere and at any time, and perfectly. Just the day before, as the gold had come finally pouring out of its destiny, Francisco Braun had killed the one link between the uranium trucks and his master. It was Francisco's idea to hire a thug to do the killing and then have him picked up. He was a murdering genius and though Francisco talked little about himself, what Caldwell had pieced together of his background confirmed that killing came naturally to Braun. He was the grandson of a Nazi war criminal who had fled to Uruguay and had joined the local police. Young Francisco, too, had joined the police, forming a squad of such ferocity that they made terrorists look pale. And then strangely one day, Francisco switched to the urban guerrilla army. And his explanation was:

"There were fewer rules as to how one killed."

Caldwell did not press further. This day, he had the three hundred thousand dollars in gold ready for Francisco. But every time he thought of paying him, his due and extra, he felt his palms grow moist with fear. Of course, he had been trained not to show it.

"Mr. Caldwell," was all Francisco had said.

"Francisco," was all Caldwell had said, sitting erect in his chair as though enthroned.

Harrison Caldwell had little flat bars made for Francisco, bars stamped with the Caldwell imprint. Three hundred thousand dollars in gold didn't even cover the leather blotter on the rosewood desk.

Francisco looked at it and clicked his heels. Caldwell wondered if one day this beautiful, deadly young man would turn on him.

"Francisco," he said, "we have a problem. I believe some people in the nuclear facility at McKeesport, Pennsylvania, are beginning to establish a trail. It is our wish, Francisco, that since we cannot cover the trail completely, the trackers be removed."

Caldwell explained that the head of security, according to his reports, had found a trail of bills of lading that led to the trucks, indicating they were full, not empty. She had with her two men of apparent superior ability.

"On this matter, Francisco, I do not want attention."

"Yes, Mr. Caldwell."

"Do you have anything against killing a woman?"

"I like women," said Francisco Braun. He said this with a smile. "I like them very much."

The proud Islamic Knights didn't like the idea of killing a woman. Or a yellow man. The white would be no problem—in fact they might do him for nothing. There was general laughter in the holy mosque temple, a former jitterbug hall in Boston. A faggy white guy was putting up a lot of bread to off three people. The proud Knights had offed people just to see if a new gun worked. A white reporter came around one day, and they told him that Hitler should have killed all the Jews and then the rest of the whites. They dug Hitler. All those uniforms and concentration camps.

When some Jews called their statement vicious and anti-semitic, the newspaper attacked the Jews. After all, blacks were now the official oppressed minority. Jews were out. Blacks were in. The paper called the Islamic Knights a positive social movement.

The faggy white guy was offering a thousand dollars now in cash, and eighty thousand dollars when they were done. They all knew what they would do. They would take the thousand, off the three, including the woman and the yellow man, take the eighty thousand dollars and then rip off the man's watch, and maybe off the man.

Some of them thought he was pretty enough to keep. They kept people, usually women, in rooms with locks. Sometimes they sold them. Sometimes they bought them. They had nothing to do with any Arab movement or any real Islamic movement, although they tried. The police called it breaking and entering when they were caught stealing a rug from a mosque. They called it reaching out for prayer understanding.

Again, the local newspaper sent down the reporter, who saw all manner of integrity in the young men. When he heard a knocking in one of the closets, he asked what it was.

"She be wantin' food. Peoples say we be doin' slavery. We gotta feed dem ladies. We gotta keep 'em in clothes. Hell, it worse than keepin' a dog." Thus spoke the exalted imam, supreme leader.

The reporter was offered the woman as a friendly gesture. He returned to write about a misunderstood group seeking free enterprise, and called for a dialogue between the Knights and community leaders. He did not mention the desperate knocking coming from the doors. Nor did he mention that the rug belonging to the real mosque of Lebanese Sunnis was being sold right before his eyes. He had the black beat, and he didn't see how mentioning those unpleasantries would have any bearing on the stories. His story was about black men with the courage to stand up to pressure groups and criticism.

Francisco Braun knew what he was buying. He was buying very sloppy killers. They probably had practiced on relatives first, then neighbors, and then branched out. Braun understood that every judge who released these killers back into the community had probably been responsible for more black deaths than any Ku Klux Klan chapter during the height of lynchings at the turn of the century.

Francisco Braun did not care. He had seen their kind in the slums of the world. They did not even make good guerrillas. If Francisco Braun were to stage a black revolution in America, he would not use these, but those middle-class blacks who struggled to build homes and send their children to school. They were soldiers. This was garbage. But garbage was what he needed. Lots of it.

"I want a massacre," said Francisco.

"De green gotta be seen, man."

"Certainly," said Francisco. He felt one of them sidle up close to him. To understand these people one had to know that a thousand dollars now was more important than a country later. They were probably thinking robbery, and possibly even male rape. Many men thought that when they saw the tender features of Francisco Braun.

Francisco smiled gently, and with a smooth, practiced motion, put a twenty-five-caliber Beretta into the bulging pants of the young man sidling up to him, and sent a slug into the bulge. There were some very pearl-white teeth grinning back at him from an asphalt-black face.

Though a pumping red ooze seeped from the crotch of his pants, the pain had yet to show in the young man's face. The grin, Francisco knew, was the first reaction, the total disbelief of what had been done. The Islamic Knights understood they were not dealing with a social worker or a reporter. They were packed into three cars by evening.

They stopped to rape and pillage a farmhouse in New Jersey until the figure of Francisco Braun appeared at the doorway.

"Keep moving," said Francisco.

In Pennsylvania the three carloads complained that they had been without entertainment for fifteen hours. They were suffering withdrawal symptoms. Francisco asked for someone to enumerate all their needs. They picked the supreme imam leader. Francisco listened to all the requests politely, then shot out his eyes. The three carloads did not stop until they reached a suburb of McKeesport, and the address Mr. Caldwell had given him.

At that point, Francisco laid out machine guns, machetes, pistols, and a few hand grenades on the hoods of the cars. The young Knights could not believe their good luck. Not only were they going to off this white, they were going to cut him into pieces.

"They're loaded," said Francisco. "In that house, down there," he said, pointing from a ridge down to a ranch house with a lit living room and three figures present around a table, "are three people without weapons. I, on the other hand, have a pistol. I can kill at least three of you before you kill me. I won't tell you which three. Now the choice is between three defenseless people who have done nothing to you, and me, a man who would like nothing better than putting blood spots on your black skin. Your choice."

And then he smiled very sweetly. It took the Islamic Knights less than a full second to decide. With a cry of holy war they grabbed their weapons and ran screaming toward the ranch house in the little valley.

Francisco Braun knew that a mass attack like this

could not be stopped. He had seen it before. No matter how bad they were, the fury of the Knights' assault, combined with numbers, would neutralize any skill. He would have liked to do the job himself, but Mr. Caldwell had stressed he wanted distance from the crime. Too bad. There was a woman there, too. He liked women. He would have liked that woman. She was so beautiful. He ached for a woman. Sadly he turned back to his car. He could not bear to watch the pack having all the fun.

Sometimes, he thought, money did not pay for all the longing in him. But he knew that working for Mr. Caldwell, there would always be more women. As Mr. Caldwell had said:

"Great wealth needs a great sword. You, Francisco Braun, are my sword. Plan on it being moist."

And Francisco knew he had found the one man he wanted to work for, knew it even as he knelt on one knee before his lord.

Sadly, Francisco got into his own car. The shooting should be starting now. He turned to his engine. Perhaps that had blocked the sound. He opened the window. Still no sound. He had given them AK-47's, an excellent field weapon, perhaps the best. Nothing. Not even a grenade going off or the sound of a machete. Francisco Braun got out of the car and looked down into the valley. An old man in flowing robes was returning into the house. Three carloads of ghetto youths lay in the driveway. There had not even been a yell. Not a cry.

Now loud sounds came from the house. A man was growling, something about cleaning up bodies. The older man, the Oriental, turned his back on the younger, the white. The white was complaining.

"If you kill them, you clean them up. There are large garbage bags in the kitchen. You can get them as well as anyone."

The younger white moved the bodies around like small cartons, stacking them as he complained about always getting the dirty work. Three carloads stacked like a pyramid.

Francisco estimated the bodies were from 170 to 270 pounds. And they flew onto the pile.

"The last time," said the white. And then, as though he had known Francisco was looking down all along, he glanced up to the hill.

"Hey, sweetheart, you want yours?" said the man.

Francisco knew he wanted that man as he had wanted no one else in the world. He wanted the young one. And he wanted the old one, and then in ultimate satisfaction he would finish off, like a dessert, the woman. They were all his now. And Mr. Caldwell could not possibly mind that he took them himself. The plan of the ghetto youths had failed.

5

Francisco Braun did not collect the reward for killing the fiercest man in Barcelona by rushing in. Granted, he could crack a man's ribs with a single karate blow. He had put out the eyes of a fleeing woman at fifty yards with a fine handgun. And she had been a fast woman, too. Even faster after she dropped her baby.

But the greatest weapons Francisco Braun had at his command were reason and patience. And he forced himself to move correctly even though his passion to take all three immediately strained him mightily. They had killed the garbage he had picked up in Boston. Physically, they moved extraordinarily well, so fast he had not been able to determine which school of hand fighting they used. He could get off a shot now. But that might be risky. He might get one and then have to hunt the others, because he did not know what these men could do. He did not know who they were, and if he did not know who they were, he just might miss. They had shown they were special, very special.

Of course, if he launched a grenade into the house now, they would probably scatter in confusion and he could pick them off. Probably. But he was not alive because of probabilities.

Besides, he had help now, a man who truly knew how to use power. And Francisco Braun knew how to use what he had. He was never one who preferred to get his hands dirty when he didn't have to.

Already he had an advantage over the two men in the house below him. He knew how dangerous they were. But they had no idea how dangerous he was, or that he was going to kill them. They couldn't even know he was there. That had always been more than enough of an edge to make Francisco victorious. There was no reason to believe it would change now. He would know them, they would not know him, and then he would kill them. He had been lucky that they had shown themselves, lucky that he had not gone in first.

He returned to the trunk of the car, took out a brief-case, and opened it to two long black lenses that clicked into each other. Then he carefully screwed them into a large frame camera, to which he attached a light but steady tripod.

It was cool in the Pennsylvania hill country, but the air was not refreshing. The stench of distant slag heaps from old coal mines created an odor like rotting coffee grounds smoldering in the center of the earth. The small house looked warm and friendly with logs burning in the fireplace of the living room. Francisco Braun focused the camera on the living room. Above the fireplace mantel was a photograph. When he could read the photographer's name in the corner of the photograph, he knew that the lens was in correctly. He moved the focus back to the door.

And then in a split second, with less concern than a carpenter hammering in the thousandth nail of a roof, Francisco Braun shot out the living-room window with a handgun that he had back in his pocket even before the echoes of the shots returned from the dark Pennsylvania hills.

The older and younger man were out of the front door before all the glass had settled, and Francisco's camera whirred off twenty-five shots in one second. By the second second, he had the camera in one hand and the door to his car open in the other. Before the third, he was driving away as fast as the car could pick up speed.

Outside McKeesport, Pennsylvania, he slowed down and took the film out of the camera. By the time he reached New York City, and the home of Mr. Caldwell, he was cruising comfortably. He called for an appointment with Mr. Caldwell. Mr. Caldwell sometimes called himself an American. But Francisco knew he had to be something else. Mr. Caldwell had never asked to be called Harrison. The problem with Americans was they wanted to be everyone's friends. Mr. Caldwell had that wonderful ability not to want that. That made working for him easier. You knew Mr. Caldwell was Mr. Caldwell. He was not your friend.

"This is Francisco Braun. I would like to see Mr. Caldwell at his convenience," Francisco said into the telephone with raised braille numbers in the dial handle. These could be punched in the dark, quite necessary because the phone was in the photographic darkroom set up in his Upper East Side New York apartment. Mr. Caldwell had put him there, with a direct-access line, the day after he had called Francisco his "sword."

"We will give an audience this afternoon," said the secretary, and Francisco got the hour, without wondering what "audience" meant. He had his pictures, twenty in less than a second, each taken faster than an eye could blink or an eardrum pick up sound.

In photography, as in the rest of life, Francisco had

learned that an advantage was always balanced by a disadvantage somewhere else. In other words, nothing was free. Despite the incredible clarity of his lenses and the large format, the high speed of his rapid shots needed a film so fast and volatile that the photographs ultimately came out with little more clarity than a child's snapshot. But that would be enough to start a search into the backgrounds of these men, if Mr. Caldwell was as powerful as he seemed. Money, after all, was power. To find out about the backgrounds of these men, Francisco would, of course, find out exactly what they could do, or where they would be or who they were. And when one built enough advantages, one struck. This for opponents who were a cut above. The rest of mankind could be dispatched at whim, at gravesides or meeting halls, or wherever.

There was a calm in the beautiful blond face of Francisco Braun as the strip of film moved through the developer and then into a rinse, and finally into the chemicals that would stop the developing process so no more light could affect the images. This would fix the negatives. With the best negatives, he would make prints, and then he would have his victims' faces set before him to study at leisure. More important, this would give him something to pass on for identification.

He liked the intricate power of Bach on stereo as he worked. It soothed the inner elements of his mind. It saved him from whistling. It set the mood. These would be extraordinary kills, not common disposals. He remembered the smooth way the Islamic Knights were dispatched. He wished he had had his camera out then. But he had not expected them to fail. There had been too many, no matter how incompetent. Incompetence, after all, was why he had chosen them.

A strange thing came up on what appeared to be the

best negatives. The face of the white appeared to be looking toward the camera. Three frames. Full face. That was an improbable fluke. Impossible, really, because no one was going to notice what was on a distant hill in one second, especially in the confusion of the aftermath of having a living-room window shot out. Francisco had seen it before—in panic and confusion the heads would bob about in every direction. Only because the camera was so fast could it appear that a person actually had noticed, then looked at, the camera. Pictures did lie.

This would always be clearer in the print, even with the lesser quality of the high-speed film Francisco used. The eyes would be open, almost dead, because they were really unfocused. The face, of course, would have the mouth wide open, because in panic, people stopped breathing through their noses and used their mouths. The body, too, would testify to the panic. The trunk would be moving in one direction and the arms flailing about in another. Of course, on this negative, it looked as though the target was somewhat composed. But that might have been due to his extraordinary ability at hand fighting, perhaps some automatic body control. Of course, he could not be composed, and that would come clear in the prints.

Francisco ran the negatives into a drum which could print before the negatives were dry. He punched in the numbers of the box that he kept close by. The box was not for film. Nor did it hold any other photographic accoutrements. Instead, it kept a single Waterford crystal glass of red wine barely chilled. Life, after all, was made up of these moments. He was always between one kill and another. Why not take the pleasure of Bach and a good Beaujolais while waiting?

Unlike most wine experts, Francisco preferred his red

wine without the customary breathing period of an hour. He liked that extra bit of sharpness. And he always had only one glass and never more. He poured the rest of the wine down the developing sink.

The drum whirred, Bach sang through the instruments over the centuries, and the red wine flowed over Francisco's tongue, then ever so gently through his body. When the drum clicked, Francisco knew two things: that the pictures were printed and that he had one-half glass left to enjoy.

With precise movements he removed the three frames, laid them out, and turned on the light.

The heavy Waterford crystal hit the floor but did not crack. The wine spilled out. And it was not the target's mouth that was open in confusion, but Francisco Braun's.

He stepped back from the developing sink. It was impossible. It had to be an accident. He forced himself back to the sink.

There, looking up at him, was a man's face perfectly focused on the camera. And the mouth was not the least bit open in terror. It was thin and rising; in fact, there was a smile on the face looking at the camera, as though Francisco Braun's threat to his life was some kind of joke. Francisco examined all three full-face pictures. In all three there were smiles.

Quickly he ran the entire twenty pictures through the print drum. He had to see everything.

He tapped his feet, waiting. He turned off the damned Bach. He told the drum to hurry. He reminded himself not to speak to inanimate objects. He told himself that Francisco Braun did not lose his discipline that easily. He reminded himself how many men he had killed. And then he kicked the crystal glass into the wall.

When the pictures appeared, they were even more

forbidding, but Francisco Braun was ready for that. The first frame captured the two as they came out of the house. In the second frame it was clear that the pair had been instantly aware of him. The old man, surprisingly, moved as well as, if not better than, the younger. In fact, the older man's gaze into the camera was the more interesting of the two. It was as though he were checking the weather. Absolutely no care whatsoever. Then he turned to the younger to make sure he had seen what was on the ridge, and seeing that the young one was already staring at the camera, he turned back into the house. And then, of course, came those three pictures, those featuring the amusement on the face and in the dark eyes focused perfectly, no panic at all.

Good. Francisco Braun had done wisely not to attack at once. He took two identifiable images, with height apparent and weight probable, and brought them with him for his appointment with Mr. Caldwell.

Mr. Caldwell's office now sprawled across an entire floor in a downtown New York City building. Two uniformed men with a crest of an apothecary jar and a sword emblazoned in red on their trim dark jackets stood at the doorway.

"I have an appointment with Mr. Caldwell," said Braun. He held the two pictures under his arm in a small leather envelope.

"Please, if you will?" said the guard.

"If I will, what?" said Braun.

"Wait for your audience."

"I am unaware that I am going to perform for anyone."

"Wait," said the guard.

There was that term "audience" again.

As soon as the doors opened, Francisco Braun began to

suspect what the guard and the secretary had been talking about.

There were no separate offices anymore. Rather, the secretaries and lesser employees sat at desks on either side of the room, leaving a vast open expanse in the middle. There, on a raised platform, was a high-backed chair. The chair glimmered with colored stones, possibly jewels. Above the chair hung the strange embossed seal, red on dark velvet. And in the chair, one hand resting on an arm, the other in his lap, was Mr. Harrison Caldwell.

"We will see you now," said Mr. Caldwell.

Francisco Braun looked around. He looked for the others. But Mr. Caldwell was alone. There wasn't anyone within twenty-five yards of him. A jeweled finger beckoned Braun up to the high-placed chair.

Braun heard his own footsteps click on the polished marble leading to the platform. Not one of the lesser employees looked up. The hand with the jeweled finger extended to Braun. He would have shaken it, except the palm was turned down. There was no doubt anymore. This was an audience, not a meeting.

"Your Majesty," said Francisco Braun, kissing the hand.

"Francisco Braun, my sword," said Harrison Caldwell. "Have you come to tell us that you have disposed of our problem?"

Braun stepped back with a bow. So Mr. Caldwell thought he was a king for some reason. True, the money was good, and Mr. Caldwell had yet to do anything foolish. But this new dimension forced Braun to consider more carefully before he spoke each word. Caldwell could be insane. Yet if he were mad, he was still awesomely rich. Even the major corporations of America, Braun knew, did not have money to waste on vast space in the financial district. This one room, this throne room, filled an entire floor.

"Your Majesty faces a more formidable enemy than I first realized."

"Enemy?"

"Yes, your Majesty," said Braun.

"We have neither permanent enemies nor permanent friends."

"Your Majesty. I did not choose these men to kill. They are not my enemies."

"As long as you serve me, Francisco, they are."

"Yes, your Majesty. They escaped the first assault," said Braun. "I have come because you have mentioned that with your power you have greater access to information than ever before."

"Greater every day," said Caldwell.

"I want to know more about these two so that I may better dispose of them for you."

"Enemies are not always enemies, you know."

Braun hesitated. He did not know if he dared correct Caldwell now. But he had to. If he were going to eliminate those two, he had to have help. If not, better to leave with one's life.

"Your Majesty, you yourself wanted them eliminated because they were interfering with something, according to your reports. Have they stopped interfering?"

"Not to our knowledge."

"Then I need help. If they are more formidable, then to hang their heads on your walls, so to speak, would give you greater respect in the eyes of men who respect only force."

"Force is not only blood, Francisco. But a good sword would think that way. So be it. We will give you what you need."

"I need, your Majesty, to identify two men," said Francisco. He unsnapped the leather folder and presented the pictures to Mr. Caldwell, or His Highness Mr. Caldwell. Braun was not sure which.

Caldwell did not take the pictures, but made Braun hold them up before him.

"I see. What contempt in that face," said Caldwell. "What an arrogant smile. He must have thought very little of the photographer. I would have, too. They are not good pictures."

"What I need to know is where they have learned what they have learned. They have special skills."

Braun held the pictures before His Majesty Mr. Caldwell. The extension of the arm pressured the nerves so that the pictures began to tremble. His Majesty Mr. Caldwell took no notice. He stared at the ceiling. Braun glanced there. It was a plain ceiling. His Majesty Mr. Caldwell must be off in his own mind, thought Braun. He lowered the pictures.

Caldwell snapped his fingers. Braun raised the pictures. Caldwell chuckled.

"An amusing idea has occurred to us," said Caldwell, who knew that his idea would not amuse Braun in the least. He lowered his eyes to meet his sword's. "Our good Francisco, do not let what I am about to say trouble you excessively. But in the days of the true monarchs, there was a person who fought the king's battles. He was called the king's champion. He was the best in the land. Our idea, the idea that amuses us, is that these two may wield powers that are greater than yours."

A bolt of anger shot through Francisco Braun. He felt like tearing the pictures away from Caldwell, this imitation king, His Highness of a court that had not existed for centuries, the old Spanish monarchy. But His Majesty Mr. Caldwell was also the richest man he had ever worked for. And up to now he had not been a fool at all.

Francisco Braun replied, with great control in an icy tone:

"All I have told your Highness is that the two men are not yet dead. But they are in the process of dying. Your sword begged his crown only to assist that process, to help establish your power in the eyes of those who would destroy you."

"Well spoken, good Francisco," said Caldwell. "We will arrange everything." With a slight beckoning motion he moved a single finger. A secretary clippety-clipped along the polished marble floors. Braun felt her come up behind him. She kissed Caldwell's feet and took the pictures.

"We will speak to you about those later," said Caldwell. The young woman nodded. Apparently she wasn't even allowed to speak to Caldwell. Braun had been given that honor.

Then Caldwell's hand came forward. Braun knew exactly what his liege wanted. He took a deep breath, kissed the ring, and backed toward the door. Before he left, an aide handed him a heavy briefcase and an address a few blocks away from Wall Street.

It was the gold exchange. He was carrying at least forty pounds of gold. Was he a delivery boy now? Was Caldwell demoting him to that? He delivered the gold to the exchange, and inside, with suppressed anger, he took bar after bar of gold out of the briefcase and slammed it on the counter.

A bespectacled old man in a vest weighed each bar, chuckling.

"Caldwell gold. A good family. Always liked dealing with the Caldwells. Real bullionists, if you know what I mean."

"Of course I don't," said Francisco. "What is a real bullionist?"

"Well, you have people who get into gold just for profit, and then you have the real old houses."

"Really. How old are the Caldwells?"

"Before the founding of America," said the old man. He took another bar to the assayer's scale. Braun looked around the room with a mild contempt. The building was heavily buttressed with steel that no one had bothered to polish for decades and a mustiness had settled on the whole place. The scale itself was old and battered, and the pans that hung from the balance bar were warped and bent. Yet if one put an exact weight on one side, one could be as sure as gravity that when the other side balanced, the weights were precisely equal.

That removed the remotest possibility of cheating.

"It's a pleasure to deal with the Caldwells," said the old man. "They know their gold. You see the Caldwell crest, you know you are not dealing with someone trying to skim a few ounces on a ton. The crest means a lot. It's an old crest, an old forge that one is."

Braun looked at his watch. He made this obvious, so the old coot would not babble on. But the man stopped only until Braun looked at him.

"See this crest," said the old man, pointing to an apothecary jar and a sword stamped into the gold itself.

"At least twenty times today," said Braun.

"That apothecary jar is the symbol for pharmacists now, but it used to be for alchemists. Do you know what an alchemist is, young man?"

"No," said Braun. He looked at the remaining bars in the bag. There were three more to be weighed. He sighed. So the money was good. So Caldwell had been extremely shrewd. Did this make up for kissing rings and delivering parcels?

"The word 'alchemist' is the root of our modern word 'chemist,' " said the old man. "It comes from the Egyptian, 'al hemist.' "

"Fantastic. I wonder if you might be able to tell me all these wonderful things about alchemists while you continue weighing the gold?"

The old man chuckled, but he did move.

"Alchemists could do everything. And did everything. Cures, potions, everything. They were so valuable that every court in Europe had one. But they got ruined. You know why?"

"Yes," said Braun. "Weigh the damned gold."

"Right. Gold. They claimed they could make gold from lead. Got them the reputation of being phonies. Soon people wouldn't hire them because they were leery of the hoodoo. You know, hocus-pocus."

"Weigh the gold," said Braun.

"And the alchemists just died off like an extinct species. But here is the strange part, and it has something to do with this crest here. Ain't a forge mark. I know forge marks."

If it is getting this bad to work for Caldwell, thought Braun, maybe it will get worse. Maybe Caldwell has a disease of the brain.

"There's those in gold today who think maybe the old alchemists really did turn lead to gold, although there's no scientific proof for it."

"Did they do it while they weighed the gold?"

"Oh, yeah, okay," said the old man, hoisting a gold bar to the empty side of the balance. The weight used as a counterbalance was made of chrome, its surface polished to perfection. If any scratches had been added to take off weight, they would show immediately.

"Well, there was this legend about the philosopher's stone. The legend was that that one stone was the secret to turning lead into gold, and it was passed along as a sort of formula. Mix lead, the stone, and some other hocus-pocus and you've got it. Presto. But, of course modern chemists proved that no stone would ever cause that kind of chemical change. Can't be done by adding any kind of a single stone.''

Braun watched the bar measure the perfect troy pound.

''But you know what some people now believe that stone was? Not a secret ingredient you added to the lead, but the keeper of the secret ingredient necessary to make gold. The alchemists wouldn't put their formula to paper because paper is something that's easy to carry off. They'd only inscribe it on something so heavy that it couldn't be stolen. Like a stone—the philosopher's stone. And for all we know, that formula could have been twenty-four-karat real. I guess I am just a boring old man, eh?''

''To know thyself,'' said Braun, ''is a virtue.''

''That's why this Caldwell crest is interesting, because it has got the mark of the sword. Do you know what the sword means? It means that for some reason they were cut off from alchemy. They could have cut the ties themselves or some king might have done it for them. Who knows?''

''I know,'' said Braun. ''I know that I do not care. Send the receipt to Mr. Caldwell. Thank you, good-bye.''

''Wait a minute. It isn't his receipt,'' said the old man, who had worked at the gold exchange more years than anyone wanted to count. ''This isn't Caldwell's gold. It's only minted by the Caldwells. It belongs to you. Mr. Caldwell has set up an account for you here at the gold exchange.''

''You mean all of that is mine?''

''Absolutely. As good as gold.''

"Ah," said Braun, who suddenly was most interested in the Caldwells, a fine old house among many fine old houses. The Caldwells had been dealing in gold in New York since it was called New Amsterdam, said the old man, and Francisco Braun told him to take his time and not leave out any of the details about these wonderful people.

Harrison Caldwell left his throne and allowed his new manservant to dress him in a dark business suit. He put on a neat striped tie and removed the large ring. Polished black shoes replaced the slippers that had been kissed repeatedly that day.

He could have assigned this task coming upon him now to an underling. But he knew that there were some things one assigned and some one did not. One never allowed someone else to be one's alchemist, nor did one allow someone else to be one's foreign minister. Of course, he was not a country yet, but what was Saudi Arabia but a family? A very rich one.

All he needed was some land. That would be easy. Because he was who he was, Harrison Caldwell knew what money could buy. Also because he was who he was, Caldwell understood clearly why no minister or alchemist could be trusted to help him fulfill his destiny. The Spanish throne had trusted, and the story of that transgression was much more than just history to Harrison Caldwell. It was *his* history.

It had almost worked. The minister had been the sword of the king. The alchemist could make gold. Unfortunately, the alchemist's feat was so expensive that it defeated its own purpose—getting the substance known as owl's teeth was so costly that to make one gold coin would cost three.

"Does the king know you can do that?" the minister asked.

"No. Not the king. I only showed it to you because you saved my daughter."

"Why not the king? He is our lord," said the minister.

"Because when the kings know you can make some gold, they always want more. And that has gotten many alchemists killed. You see, kings think they can find owl's teeth. But they can't. And then they insist you use something else, and then, of course, you die."

"What if I told you that if you will make a few coins for our king, I can make sure you will never be harmed?"

"In our lore you can find many accounts of kings who have promised that, but none who has kept it. Kings just do not know their own limits."

"What if I told you I would set those limits? If you make me a few coins for the king, I will make you rich and assure you no king will ever ask you to do what you cannot do."

"How can you assure me that?"

"I will be king," said the king's minister. "I will use his greed to take his throne."

"No. Don't you see? My life is in danger already. Lords are forgiven by other lords, but alchemists are killed like useless dogs when they've fulfilled their purpose."

"I will marry your daughter. Is that enough proof? She will be my queen. Would a king kill his father-in-law? You will be noble too."

"It is a great risk."

"Life is risk," said the minister. "But your daughter could be queen."

"Marry her first," said the alchemist.

"Done," said the minister.

What happened then would be passed throughout the ages from each Caldwell family elder to each Caldwell son.

Harrison Caldwell remembered his father telling him the story in their bullionist's shop late one night on his thirteenth birthday when everyone else was gone. His father had been teaching him gold, and he was old enough, his father said, to understand where the family came from.

The minister married the alchemist's daughter and they produced a son. Upon the birth of that child, the alchemist made a purchase, investing in the very expensive ingredient that was so rare it took three years to find and five times the amount of gold it could make to buy. But buy it they did, from a place deep within the land where the Negro lived, the land now known as Africa.

And before the king's eyes, Harrison Caldwell's ancestor made the gold from lead. The king was so impressed he wanted to see more. And this time, the special alchemist's ingredient cost only four times what the gold was worth. And the alchemist found the source within one year.

The king was sure he saw a pattern. The secret alchemist's ingredient cost five times gold at first and took three years to get. The second batch cost four times as much and took only one year to get. Eventually, like all commodities that start out expensive in their acquisition, the more one bought, the less it would cost. So thought the king who looked forward to the day that the price of owl's teeth became much less than that of gold itself.

Indeed, he was right. The next batch cost three times

the price of gold and was there in six months. And the next shipment, far larger still, cost twice as much and was ready in a month.

But what the king did not know was that only the first time, under the instruction of the foreign minister, did his alchemist make gold from lead.

The other times he only melted and recast part of the gold. Only the first time was he able to obtain the magic ingredient. Only the first time did the king watch the lead transform. His foreign minister had convinced him it would be unseemly to look so greedy, to actually stand over the alchemist like some merchant.

Ultimately, the king came to believe that if he made enough gold it would be cheaper to produce than the gold itself. For every coin paid, he would get three in return.

"We have turned the corner. We now can be the richest kingdom in all Europe. With all this gold we will rule the world, as we should," said the monarch, who promptly emptied almost the entire treasury to buy massive amounts of the rare ingredient that made gold.

Harrison Caldwell remembered his father pointing out that this was where everything went wrong. Now the king, expecting to be the richest man in the world, hired a famous murderer to sit by his side, a man from a foreign land. The king feared that his great wealth would draw more enemies to him than ever before. He wanted to be ready for them. This murderer was especially sly and followed the alchemist by some magic which did not let the alchemist see him. And he observed that the alchemist did not make gold at all.

The minister got word of this and fled with his wife and son and as much gold as he could. The alchemist took the philosopher's stone. They sailed free of the Spanish coast, but almost as soon as they were out of sight of land, a storm struck the ship. The weight of the stone and the weight of the gold provided too much ballast, and the ship sank. The alchemist and his daughter were lost. But the minister and son escaped with a small chest of gold.

Eventually they made it to New Amsterdam, which later became New York City, and there, with the meager gold they had saved, they established their house. And they took the name Caldwell. And so Harrison Caldwell learned, on his thirteenth birthday, where the gold was, where the stone was, and to whom the gold and stone belonged. He learned, as had every male heir throughout the family's history, how the Caldwells had almost become kings, and what their bullionist's mark of the apothecary jar and the sword meant.

Perhaps it was because Harrison was a daydreamer, perhaps because he was sickly and did not get along well with other boys, but it was he who vowed to make the legend a reality. He would find the stone and make gold again.

"What makes you think you can succeed where the rest of us only hoped?"

"Because ninety percent of the scientists who ever lived are alive today. Today is different."

"The world doesn't change, Harrison."

"When it comes to people, I'm counting on that, Dad," said Harrison.

He was sure that with the advantage of modern equipment and access to so many great thinkers, the time had come to use the old family map and get the formula for the stone.

It was a godsend that the missing ingredient turned out to be uranium. The world was loaded with it now. And because people hadn't changed, Harrison Caldwell had found a way to make sure that he would never get caught while stealing it.

In his business suit with the photographs of the two men his sword had given him, Harrison Caldwell, who was more and more understanding his destiny, met in one of his business offices a gentleman from Washington.

The man thanked him for helping him buy his house. Caldwell said that was nothing. Anyone would help a friend.

The man thanked him for making sure his daughter got into an exclusive school even though her grades were not good enough.

A mere nothing, answered Harrison Caldwell.

The man said, however, he was not sure that it was totally ethical for Caldwell to open up an account for him at the gold exchange.

Nonsense, answered Harrison Caldwell.

"Do you really think it's all right?" asked the man.

"I most certainly do," said Harrison Caldwell to the director of the Nuclear Control Agency. "And by the way, were these two gentlemen the ones you warned me about, the ones who were getting in the way?"

He pushed the two photographs forward across the table.

"I think so. I think they are the ones at the McKeesport site right now. I think they are plants by some agency I have yet to discover."

"You don't worry about that. I am sure I can trace them," said Caldwell, his dark Spanish eyes flashing with the joy of battle. "I will get the best information money can buy."

6

Consuelo Bonner saw the bodies outside her house. She saw the bullet hole in the window. She felt her head grow light while the skyline grew dark, like winter.

If she were not dreaming, she would swear Remo and Chiun were arguing over who should clean up the bodies, as though they were garbage to be taken out. If she were not dreaming, she would have thought the Oriental really had explained to her:

"I have done so much for him, and yet he still tries to make me a servant."

She would have also sworn Remo had answered:

"He never does his bodies."

She asked them to please throw some very cold water on her.

"Why?" asked Remo.

"So I will wake up."

"You are awake," said Chiun. "But even I would not dream of such ingratitude."

"They were trying to kill you," said Remo.

Consuelo nodded. She went to the window where the bullet hole was, and rubbed a finger over it to feel the edges of the hard glass. Remo looked on. She glanced back to him.

"I know," she said. "We must be getting close to them in some way. They don't try to kill you unless you're a danger to them."

"Or unless they made a mistake," said Remo.

"Or something else," said Consuelo.

"What else?" said Remo.

"This is my nuclear plant. My responsibility."

"You mean you don't want to admit you need us this much."

"Don't patronize me," said Consuelo. "I will do what any man does."

"Then why aren't you running for your life?"

"Because if I ran they would say I ran because I am a woman. I do not run." She steadied herself against the window. "I do not run. I do not run. I do not run."

Chiun noticed this courage in the woman. She was not Korean, and who knew who her family was, but she did have courage. She also had the failing of so many women in this country. In trying to show they were as good as men, they tried to be what most men never were. They tried to be what men thought they were.

Then again, all whites were crazy. What were they doing in this country to begin with? Working for mad Emperor Harold W. Smith who never attempted anything honorable like seizing the throne, never asked for services that would accrue to the honor of Sinanju, never provided Chiun with anything he could inscribe in the histories.

How did one pass on to future Masters of Sinanju that one acted like a storeroom guard for an emperor one did not understand?

And who would there be to pass on to if Remo did not have a child?

Chiun watched the white woman closely. He would, of course, prefer a Korean for Remo, one from Sinanju. But Remo had not been able to see the true beauty in the fairest maidens of Sinanju, seeing only their physical properties instead of how good they would be to the child and of course to Chiun.

"What do you think?" asked the white woman. "Do you think we are getting closer?" She was looking at Chiun. She had black hair, that was good. But the eyes were blue. And the skin was so pale, like clouds in the sky.

"I think I would like to meet your parents," said Chiun.

"They're dead," said Consuelo, puzzled.

"Then never mind," said Chiun. He was no longer interested in Consuelo for Remo. There was no longevity in the family. Her parents might have died in accidents, of course. But then that would only mean they were accident-prone.

"What did he mean by that?" said Consuelo.

"Never mind," said Remo. "You don't want to know."

"You don't treat him kindly," she said.

"You don't know him. I know him and I love him. So don't get involved. Besides, your life is on the line."

"You want me not to report this to the police, don't you?"

"It would help."

"Help what?"

"Keeping you alive. Someone tried to kill you. We can keep you alive. Don't bet on the police doing that."

"What policeman is going to believe that bunch out there killed themselves in a gang fight and then stacked themselves up neatly for the garbage removal?"

"Tell them we stacked them for you."

"But weren't all those young men out there killed by hand? Won't they be suspicious? I know that if I were a policeman I would be reporting something like this as unusual."

"Don't worry," said Remo. "It'll work."

As Consuelo predicted, the homicide detectives of McKeesport were suspicious. Under normal circumstances this might have caused the investigators some confusion. But since their department had recently received instructions to report any deaths like this one—deaths caused by "no apparent weapon"—to a central bureau, the detectives' next move was clear. They would pass the buck.

What none of the police knew was that their report did not end up at the FBI but at Folcroft Sanitarium, where Harold W. Smith saw the computer flag the whereabouts of Remo and Chiun. He was the one who had the request issued to every police department in the country, not so much to keep track of Remo and Chiun as to make the local police believe someone was tracking the strange deaths nationwide. Smith didn't want local cops getting together and comparing notes; that might cause an outcry. There had been so many bodies, so many criminal bodies, that the liberal press could have had a lifetime supply of martyrs.

And it would be just as dangerous if there was an outcry in favor of such killings as there would be if it were against. It would attract attention. And that was the last thing the organization could afford.

But Smith paid little attention this morning to the McKeesport report. Something was happening in America, and he was getting only inklings of it. He could not prove it yet, but someone was building another country somewhere in America. Appearing on the

computer screen was a network of people who were
stockpiling the one resource that could build an
empire—gold. Breaking down all the statistics, one could
see they were already powerful enough to form an
independent nation. Smith focused on that this morning.
Remo and Chiun would be all right. They were always
all right. The problem was never their survival. It was
the country's.

Two days later, Consuelo Bonner began recognizing
things. She recognized the subjects of the photographs
that were spread across her desk. She recognized the
badge of the man who handed her the pictures. He was
from the Nuclear Control Agency. Last but not least, she
recognized beauty. The man was beautiful. He had hair
so blond it was almost white. His eyes were the lightest
blue and his skin was as fair as snow. She would have
called him handsome, but "handsome" was not nearly
fine enough a description. His name was Francisco. He
asked if she had Spanish ancestry too, because her name
was Consuelo.

"You have the regal bearing of Spanish nobility," he
said.

"You can put away your badge," she said. She had
never wondered before what a man looked like nude,
but she did now. And she wondered what his child
would look like if she bore it.

But most of all she wondered what he was doing with
pictures of Remo and Chiun. They obviously were taken
at a great distance because of the plane compression of a
telephoto lens. They were obviously taken with high-
speed film. The images were so grainy they were barely
discernible. Remo was smiling as though posing for a
family snapshot.

"Have you seen these men?"

"Why do you ask?"

"We suspect they are dangerous."

"Why?"

"They kill people."

"That can be very safe if they kill the right people," said Consuelo.

"Spoken with wisdom, senorita," said Braun. "You should know that the Nuclear Control Agency has been watching your efforts. We don't blame you for the missing materials."

"I didn't know that," said Consuelo.

"They are looking to recommend you for a much higher position, one never before held by a woman."

"It's their loss if no woman ever held that position before."

Braun raised his hands in hurried agreement. "Absolutely. Absolutely. Of course women should hold these posts. And you will show the world just what women can do."

Consuelo looked at the pictures again.

"If I told you I knew these men, what would you do?"

"Ah, a good question. They are very dangerous, after all."

"What would you do?"

"What would you wish us to do? You are in charge of your security. We are only here to warn you about things, dangerous things like these two killers."

"I would want you to do nothing," said Consuelo.

"May I ask why?"

"If I told you, that would be telling you definitely I have seen them."

"You have already told me that," said Braun. He sat with relaxed grace in a chair before her desk. Consuelo had furnished her office without any frilly decorations. All the chairs and desks were cold and drab. The beautiful Francisco looked out of place.

Consuelo in her dark power suit, as she liked to call it, had dressed herself as she had furnished the office: starkly.

"I haven't told you anything," she said.

Braun noticed that she smiled too much. Buttoned a button that was already buttoned several times. Crossed her legs too much. Moistened her lips and then forced herself to be professional by drying them. He saw her struggling with herself.

He rose from his chair and walked to her. He put a hand on her shoulder.

"Don't do that," she said. She did not remove his hand.

He lowered his cheek to hers. She could feel the smoothness of his flesh next to hers. She could sense his body, smell the fragrance of his breath.

His whisper tickled her ear.

"I am only here to help you," he said.

She swallowed.

"I am a security officer. I will not be treated any differently from a man." She said this with firmness in her voice, but she did not move away from his hands. One of them played with the top button of her suit.

"I make love to men also," said Francisco.

"Oh," she said.

"And women," he said.

"Oh," she said.

"You are very beautiful," he said.

"I was thinking that about you," she said.

"I will do nothing you do not tell me to do."

"Then you will not harm them?"

"I will not seek to have them arrested in any way. All I

want is to know where they are. They are with you, aren't they?''

''Yes. I am using them to protect me.''

''Fine. Where are they now?''

''Nearby.''

Consuelo felt the smooth cheek leave her, the beautiful hands leave the folds of her suit. Francisco Braun straightened up.

''Where?'' he asked sharply.

''Nearby. We're all going to La Jolla, California.''

''Why there? You must protect your plant here in Pennsylvania.''

Shaken from her trance by Francisco's sudden withdrawal, Consuelo refused to divulge what she had found out.

''You only asked to be informed where they were.''

''There is no law against you telling me more,'' said Francisco. He glanced behind him. He had to make sure they were not in the room. ''Remember I can guarantee you your promotion if you cooperate. Ask your superior. Ask the head of the agency.''

She did. She waited until he had shut the door behind him and then recovered her senses. Immediately she ran a check on him and was glad she did. The head of the NCA not only verified what Francisco had told her but also ordered her to render him any assistance he asked for. He also told her he was happy with her work.

''I'm glad, because when you lose as much uranium as this plant has, sometimes people tend to blame the security officer.''

''We know how good you are, Ms. Bonner. We are not an agency that throws blame around.''

''I hope you do throw credit, because I think I am onto something very hot. I think I am going to break this case.''

"How?"

"You'll see when I do it."

Consuelo, Remo, and Chiun arrived in La Jolla the next morning. Consuelo thought she had never seen such beautiful houses so tastefully set against such perfect scenery. Remo said La Jolla had the best weather in America. It was always spring in this beautiful little city by the Pacific. Chiun noted that there were too many whites.

"It would be nicer if there were more Koreans," said Chiun.

"If there were more Koreans it would look like a fishing village," said Remo.

"What is wrong with fishing villages?" said Chiun.

"I've seen Sinanju. Though it is by the water, it is definitely not as nice as La Jolla."

"I'll do the questioning," said Consuelo. "This is the first break in the case."

"It's all yours," Remo said. He wondered what it would be like to live around here. He wondered what it would be like to own a home and live in one place with a family he belonged to. He wondered what it would be like to have his own car, to park in his own garage, and go to sleep in the same bed every night.

One person who did not have to worry about living in La Jolla was James Brewster, recently retired from the McKeesport nuclear facility.

He had worked all his life as a dispatcher for one power facility or another, retiring early from McKeesport with a pension of twelve thousand dollars a year.

With that pension he had just purchased a $750,000 condominium in La Jolla, California, a retirement home.

The mortgage company had contacted the McKeesport

facility to get a reference for a rather large mortgage. They were willing to give it to someone who had only twelve thousand dollars provable income, because he was putting down a half million dollars.

James Brewster was the dispatcher who ordered the last missing uranium shipment down Kennedy Boulevard in Bayonne. James Brewster was also Consuelo Bonner's lead to breaking the case. Obviously the thieves had reached this man. And she was going to reach him too.

"He's mine," said Consuelo as they entered what appeared to be the back of an exquisite town house. They could hear the Pacific on the other side. "I want this to be legal and official. No rough stuff. Do you hear me?"

"What does she mean by rough stuff?" said Chiun, who was never rough.

"She means that we can't help with the questioning. We have laws in this country about how you question people. She wants to get admissible evidence," said Remo.

There were three apartments in the town house condominium. Brewster's name appeared above one button on the brass entrance plaque. Chiun looked around. It was a modest dwelling which of course lacked the true Korean warmth.

Chiun considered Remo's incomprehensible explanation. "What is admissible evidence?" he asked, afraid he was getting into that strange unfathomable tangle of doctrine that made Americans act crazy.

"Well, you can't get evidence by violating the law. The judge won't allow it."

"Even if what you're trying to prove is true?" asked Chiun.

"It doesn't matter if the evidence is true or not or

whether the person is guilty or not. If you don't follow the rules, the judge won't allow the evidence to decide the case."

"Truth does not matter, then?" asked Chiun.

"Well, yeah, it does. It does. But the people have to be protected from the police too. Otherwise you have a police state, a dictatorship, a tyranny," said Remo, who could have told Chiun this twisted justice was the whole reason for the organization's being, but Chiun would never have understood that one. He simply refused to.

"There have been some wonderful tyrants, Remo. Never speak against tyrants. Tyrants pay well. In the history of Sinanju, we have been honored by many tyrants."

"Tyrants have a bad name in this civilization," said Remo.

"Which is why we do not belong here. What are you doing running after this metal that has been stolen, like some slave guarding a storehouse? In a tyranny an assassin is respected."

"Shhh," said Consuelo. She rang the buzzer.

"No rough stuff," said Chiun, looking around for a sane person to share this absurdity with. Of course, there was none. Just Remo and Consuelo. Chiun was, as ever, alone in his sanity.

"Who is it?" came the voice.

"Hello," said Consuelo. "My name is Consuelo Bonner, and we are from the McKeesport facility."

"Who is the funny-looking guy?"

"His name is Remo," said Chiun.

"I mean the other," said Brewster. Chiun looked around. There was no one else in the lobby. But he knew that before he looked. Chiun examined the perfect fingernails that reflected his inner grace, reexamined his perfect presence, and knew without looking that his face was the true reflection of joy and health and nobility.

They were dealing with a person suffering either sight or judgment problems. Possibly both.

"I'm busy," said Brewster.

Remo folded his arms. He remembered his days as a policeman. There were certain forms Consuelo had to adhere to, restrictions on what to ask, and most of all prohibitions against threats. He would let Consuelo have all the rope she wanted.

"I would advise you to talk to us."

"I'm not going to talk to you without my lawyer. I want my lawyer."

"We just wish to question you."

"No lawyer, no talk."

They waited by the buzzer until a young man in his mid-twenties arrived. He had dark curly hair and a frenzied look. He charged Remo and Chiun with brutality.

"We're down here. Brewster is upstairs. How can we brutalize him?" asked Remo.

"Brutality by threats of stance," said the young man. He wore a very expensive suit, jogging shoes, and the eager look of an up-and-comer just a few years out of law school. His name was Barry Goldenson. He gave Remo a card.

"We are just here to talk to your client," said Consuelo. "My name is Consuelo Bonner, and I am in charge of security for the McKeesport nuclear facility. Your client is a former dispatcher for us. We want to find out about certain uranium shipments."

"My client will not testify against himself."

Then why talk to him? wondered Chiun. Of course, that was a logical question; therefore, it was a question not worth asking. When one began trying to apply reason to these people, one began unraveling seaweed.

Barry Goldenson led Consuelo, Remo, and Chiun up to a very small living room. There was a bedroom, and one bathroom and a small kitchen.

"You paid three-quarters of a million dollars for this?" asked Remo.

"He got in before the big price jump," said Goldenson. "This is a bargain for La Jolla."

"What do you get for a hundred thousand?" asked Remo.

"Parking," answered Brewster. He was of average height with a graying mustache and a new tan. He wore an open shirt with a gold chain nestled in a forest of gray chest hair. On the chain hung a gold pendant. He sat back in the full comfort of a man with every confidence in his safety.

"I could get everything you want out of him and his lawyer in thirteen seconds," Remo whispered to Consuelo.

Consuelo shot him a dirty look.

"Now, Mr. Brewster, you were the dispatcher who sent a shipment of uranium that disappeared. In fact, you sent several shipments that disappeared."

"My client does not have to answer that."

"We have his name on the order. We have his pay records. We have his countersigned receipts. We have statements from others in the plant."

"Are you persecuting him for doing his job?" said Goldenson.

"Would you care to explain how he amassed a half-million dollars on a salary that for most of his life was ten thousand dollars? It only rose above that in the last few years. Would you care to explain how on a pension of twelve thousand a year this man can buy a three-quarter-of-a-million-dollar condominium?"

"America is a land of opportunity," said Goldenson.

"So after sending several shipments along some very odd routes, like Kennedy Boulevard in Bayonne, New Jersey, he's suddenly able to buy this condominium? Come on, Mr. Goldenson—nothing of value is in Bayonne, New Jersey," said Consuelo.

"Perhaps that's why he sent them through there."

"Perhaps that is why he suddenly opened a gold-bullion account after the first shipment and received a deposit of one-quarter of a million dollars immediately. Perhaps that is why every time a shipment got lost his account rose by a quarter of a million dollars." Consuelo shot the questions at both Brewster and the lawyer. She was cold and professional.

Brewster sweated.

"A man has a right to prepare for his retirement. He has a right to his golden years," said Goldenson.

"Not that golden," said Consuelo.

"Are you placing limits on a person's aspirations? America is a land of hope," said Goldenson.

Remo tapped his feet, annoyed. He wanted to know who gave Brewster the gold payoffs for shipping the uranium on those strange routes. Once he got that he could get to the person behind it all. No matter how many layers of protection there were, he could always keep cracking them until he got to the source. He stepped out onto the balcony that overlooked a magnificent view of a benign, warm ocean. Chiun did not join him. He stayed inside with the lawyer, Consuelo, and the suspect. Remo was sure he didn't understand a word of the conversation.

At worst, maybe a few crooks got away. But basically

in America, more than anywhere else in the world, the people were protected from their government. That would always be the difference between Chiun and him. To Chiun, a government, any kind of government, was only as good as its treatment of the House of Sinanju. Remo could understand that. Sinanju was poor. But Remo was not brought up poor. There was always food; and once you had food and shelter, you wanted something else. You wanted things that only America could give. It was a good country, Remo thought. He was glad he did what he did, even if sometimes it seemed as though he was really swimming against a strong current.

Expensive boats dotted the placid ocean. Out on the horizon, he noticed a glint of sun off glass. Somehow the glass was steady on a rocking boat. Everything moved with the sea but that reflection. Remo glanced back into the room.

The lawyer seemed to be handling Consuelo rather well until Chiun stepped in. The Master of Sinanju started talking to the lawyer, asking him questions. Consuelo, losing her head, ordered Chiun to be quiet.

Remo stepped back inside the room. He tried to explain to Consuelo that that was not the right way to communicate with Chiun, that indeed she might get off the first sentence, but she might not get a chance to complete the second. Consuelo answered she could not be threatened.

Goldenson winked to his client. Chiun ignored Consuelo. He spoke directly to Goldenson.

"Does your mother know you are wearing sneakers?" asked Chiun. Remo looked out the window quite intently. He was pretending he didn't know this man. Consuelo almost threw her notes into the trashcan. Chiun ignored them both. Brewster smiled, confident.

"Does she?" asked Chiun.

Goldenson looked to Consuelo and his clients as if to say, "Who is this lunatic?"

"Does she?" asked Chiun.

"I don't know if she knows what I wear for shoes," said Goldenson. There was a condescending smirk.

"If I may get on with the questioning," said Consuelo.

"Of course," said Goldenson.

"Does she?" asked Chiun.

"Please continue your questioning," said Goldenson, concentrating on ignoring the Oriental.

"Does she?" asked Chiun.

"Why don't you phone her and ask," said Goldenson. Brewster laughed and patted his lawyer on the back. Consuelo just sighed. In Korean, Remo said to Chiun: "Little father, this young man is obviously as good a criminal lawyer as money can buy. You can't get anywhere with him by speaking to him like a child. He's a tough legal adversary for Consuelo here. You don't know anything about American law. Please. Let her handle it. As a favor."

"What is her phone number?" Chiun asked Goldenson.

"Really," said Goldenson.

"Can I go out for a swim now?" asked Brewster. As far as he was concerned the danger was over.

"I cannot continue," Consuelo told Remo.

"What is her number?"

"Do you really want it?" asked Barry Goldenson. He adjusted his seven-thousand-dollar Rolex watch.

Chiun nodded. Laughing, Barry Goldenson, Esquire, gave Chiun a number with a Florida exchange.

Chiun dialed the number.

"I am going to die of shame," said Consuelo. She didn't have to ask Brewster to hang around. He decided to stay for the amusement. There wasn't anything

funnier than this going on in La Jolla, anyhow. This
Oriental was phoning the mother of one of the top
criminal lawyers in the state.

"Hello, Mrs. Goldenson?" said Chiun. "You don't
know me and I am not important. I'm calling about your
son . . . No. He is not in any trouble or danger. No, I
don't know what kind of women he is going with. . . . I
am calling about something else. I can tell that such a
fine boy has to have been raised with care. I understand
that because I have had troubles with raising a boy
myself."

Chiun looked at Remo. Remo was now rooting for the
young criminal lawyer. Remo was also rooting for the
woman to hang up on Chiun. Remo was happy to root
for anyone but Chiun.

"Oh, yes. . . . You try and try, but when your loved
one ignores your needs to fend . . . Oh, yes . . . The entire
family treasure for generations back . . . missing and
I only asked for a little help in looking . . . but that's
my problem, Mrs. Goldenson. . . . Your son can still
be helped because I know you have taught him right
. . . a nothing . . . a little thing . . . successful lawyer,
Mrs. Goldenson, and such a success should not be
wearing . . . I hate to say it . . . I won't say it . . . you don't
want to hear it . . . sneakers."

Chiun was quiet a moment, then handed the telephone to Goldenson. Goldenson adjusted the vest of his
three-piece suit and cleared his throat.

"Yes, Mother," he said. "He's not a nice man,
Mother. I am on an important case and he is on the other
side. They do things, anything to distract . . . Mother . . .
he is not a nice man . . . you don't know him . . . you
haven't seen him . . . As a matter of fact, I happen to be
wearing what many California businessmen wear for

the comfort of their feet. . . . Do you know who wears jogging shoes in courtrooms? Do you know the famous . . ."

Goldenson clenched the receiver as his face flushed. He broke eye contact with everyone in the room. Finally he handed the receiver to Chiun.

"She wants to talk to you."

"Yes, Mrs. Goldenson. I hope I didn't cause you any worry. You're welcome, and if I ever get to Boynton Beach, Florida, I will be happy to see you. No, there is nothing I can do with my son. The treasure is lost but he thinks someone else's useless metal is worth more than the family history. What can you do?"

And then Chiun offered the phone to Goldenson, asking if he had anything more to say. Goldenson shook his head. He opened his briefcase and quickly wrote out a check. He handed it to Brewster.

"This is your retainer."

"Where are you going?"

"Shoes. I am going to get a pair of dark leather shoes. Thank you, Mr. Chiun," said Goldenson bitterly.

"What about me?" asked Brewster. "Who's going to look after me?"

"Try your former employer, Ms. Bonner."

"A good boy," Chiun said to Goldenson as he left.

With Goldenson on the way it took Bonner exactly seven minutes to have Brewster sweating and making up alibis. Finally she warned him that anything further he said might be used against him and warned him not to leave La Jolla. An arrest warrant would be sworn out that very afternoon.

Before they left, Remo glanced back out at that strange reflection on the water. It hadn't moved. Other boat windows bobbed and pitched with the gentle swells of the Pacific. That reflection did not. And then Remo knew why.

On board the boat, beneath the deck, Francisco Braun checked the large gyroscope. The heavy spinning wheel kept his electron telescope balanced as steady as in a laboratory. The boat could pitch and rock, but the telescope set on that gyroscope would never move from the level created by the force of the motion.

This telescope could expand a thumbprint at two miles. It could also aim a small cannon.

Francisco Braun had seen all he had to see back in McKeesport. He had seen enough to know what would not work. A mere few hundred yards was not enough distance between Braun and his prey, against the white man and the ancient Oriental. The speed and reflexes of those two men were dangerous at that range. But launching a shell into a shorefront condominium from several miles out, where a boat was just a dot on the horizon, was like launching a shell from nowhere. If they couldn't see it, they couldn't avoid it. The key was staying beyond their awareness. And that meant distance.

He focused on the condominium until he could see the weathering on the wood, and then he lifted his sights to the second-floor balcony and the apartment of James Brewster. Consuelo and the two men should be there now.

Braun focused on the railing on the second floor. A hand rested on the railing. It was a man's hand. He had thick wrists, just like the white at McKeesport. Behind him, a kimono caught a breeze. The kimono was inside the apartment. That would be the Oriental.

Braun raised the level of the telescope. He picked up the buttons of the white man's shirt. He picked up the

Adam's apple. The chin. The mouth. It was smiling at him. So were the eyes.

Francisco Braun did not fire his gun.

7

Consuelo Bonner got a policeman, who got a judge, who gave an arrest warrant, and then she, Remo, Chiun, the policeman, and the warrant went to the condominium of James Brewster to read him his rights and place him under arrest. All according to the law.

"This is justice," said Consuelo.

The policeman rang the buzzer.

The camera stared its one thick glass eye down at the foursome.

"Justice," said Chiun to Remo in Korean, "is when an assassin is paid for his work. Justice is when the treasures of those labors, stolen while the assassin is gone, are recovered. That is justice. This is running around with papers."

"I thought you said the real treasures of Sinanju were in the histories of the Masters, that it was not the gold or the jewels or other tributes but who we are and how we became that way that make us rich," said Remo in the same language.

"Will you two stop talking, please? This is an official act of the La Jolla Police Department," said the patrolman.

"No crueler blow than to have one's own words twisted and then thrown back."

"How are they twisted?"

"Badly twisted," said Chiun.

"How?"

"It will be recorded in the histories that I, Chiun, was Master when the treasures were lost. But it will be recorded most that you, Remo, did not aid in their recovery. Instead, you served your own kind during a moment of crisis in the House of Sinanju."

"The world was ready to go. If there is no world, if everything is in some form of nuclear winter, what would the treasure of Sinanju be worth then?"

"Even more," said Chiun.

"To whom?" said Remo.

"I don't argue with fools," said Chiun.

The policeman, having determined he could neither stop the two from talking in that strange language nor get an answer from the buzzer, did according to the rights of his warrant proceed to enter said domicile of one James Brewster.

But the door was locked. He was going to send for assistance in breaking into said domicile when Remo grabbed the handle and turned. There was a snap of breaking metal. The door opened.

"Cheap door," said the La Jolla patrolman. He saw a piece of the cracked lock on the other side of the door. He bent to pick it up and then quickly let go. It was hot.

"Whadya do to the door? What happened here?"

"I let you in," said Remo. "But it won't do any good. He's not there."

"Don't be so negative. If there is one thing I have learned in criminology it is that a negative mind produces nothing. You have to think positive."

"If I thought it was snowing outside, it still wouldn't be snowing," said Remo. "He's not there."

"How do you know he's not there? How can you say he's not there?" ranted Consuelo Bonner. "How do you know until you go up and see? I am a woman but I am just as competent as any man. Don't go fouling my case on me."

"He's not there. I don't know how I know but he's not there. Believe me, he's not there. Okay?" said Remo. And he didn't know how he knew. He knew that others couldn't sense when someone was in a room behind a door. But he could no more tell her how he knew than he could tell her how light worked.

"Let me explain," said Chiun. "We are all part of a being. We only think we are disconnected because our feet are not rooted in the earth. But we are all connected. Some people have obliterated the sense of that connection but Remo and the room from which the man has left are joined in being."

"I prefer 'I dunno,' " said Consuelo.

"You people part of some cult?" asked the policeman.

"Who are these lunatics?" asked Chiun.

"Normal Americans," said Remo.

"That explains it," said Chiun.

James Brewster, of course, was not in the room.

He was at the airport with a sudden good friend. A man who looked Swedish and spoke as though he were Spanish. James Brewster never trusted good luck. But this good luck came when he couldn't afford not to trust.

He had sat trembling on a couch, his expensive lawyer having abandoned him, facing jail, disgrace, humiliation, cursing himself for ever thinking he could have gotten away with it.

When the phone began to ring he did not answer it.

"It's here. It's come apart. I'm done for. It. That's it. It." He poured himself a tumbler of Scotch.

"I took a chance. I lost. Done for."

There was a knock on the door. He didn't answer it. Let the police get him. He didn't care. A man's voice with a Spanish accent came through the door. It begged to be let in. It begged to save him.

"It's no use," sobbed James Brewster. Done. It was all over.

"You're a fool. You could be rich and live with servants beyond your wildest dreams."

"That's how I got into this pickle," said Brewster. He looked at the wall. Better get used to looking at a wall for the rest of your life, he told himself.

"You took a chance. You won. You will win even more."

"I want to go home."

"To McKeesport, Pennsylvania?"

James Brewster thought about that a moment. Then he opened the door.

He expected a Spaniard. But an incredibly beautiful blond man in a white suit stood in the doorway. He wore a dark blue shirt and a single gold chain under it, hiding a medallion of sorts.

"My name is Francisco. I have come to keep you out of jail. To give you an even richer, more splendid life than you have ever known before."

James Brewster stood in the doorway waiting. He tapped his foot, waiting.

"What are you waiting for?" asked Braun.

"To wake up," said Brewster. "This is a bad dream."

Francisco Braun slapped him across the face.

"Okay," said Brewster, his left cheek stinging like a swarm of bees had just struck him. "Awake. I'm awake."

"You are going to go to jail if you don't listen to me," said Braun.

"Very awake," said Brewster. "Really awake."

"But I can give you wealth and luxury beyond your wildest dreams."

"Asleep again. Dreaming," said Brewster. "All done. Life is over."

"I will help you get away. You can live in hiding for the rest of your life," said Braun.

"Waking up."

"Fly to Brazil. No one can arrest you in Brazil. They do not have an extradition treaty with anyone. Many criminals live a high wonderful life in Rio. You have no doubt, señor, heard of wonderful Rio."

"Almost everything I have is in this condominium."

"I will buy it."

"Well, considering land values, I think I really want to hold on to it a little longer. This isn't the right time to sell."

"Are you joking, señor? You must sell. Or go to jail."

"I didn't want you to think you could get this for a bargain price. No one should ever sell real estate in desperation."

"I will give you in gold whatever you think it is worth."

James Brewster named a price that would have purchased half the town. Considering the town was La Jolla, it was higher than the net worth of two-thirds of the members of the United Nations.

They settled on a minuscule fraction. A million dollars in gold. It came to slightly over two hundred pounds. In two valises. For which he paid extra in baggage charges at the airport.

"I know Brazil. It is a beautiful country," said Braun.

"But you must know how to handle people." Braun rubbed his fingers together. Bribes were his kind of psychology.

Brewster understood bribes. That was how he got here.

"You must know how to protect yourself," said Braun. "What if they follow your trail?"

"But you said they couldn't extradite me."

"Ah, that is the problem with your situation. You see, you helped steal uranium."

"Shhhh," said Brewster. He looked around the airport.

"No one cares. This is a busy airport. Listen. You must know how to lose a tail, even if it comes from a government seeking revenge for your helping to steal atomic materials."

"Yes. Yes. Lose a tail. Lose a tail," said Brewster.

"When you get to Rio, you hire a boat to go up the Amazon. And use your correct name."

"I hate jungles."

"I don't blame you. That is why James Brewster will go up the Amazon but Arnold Diaz will live in luxury in another condominium. And for a mere quarter of a million dollars you will have space. All the space you want."

"Only a quarter of a million?"

"And you can hire servants for three dollars a week. Beautiful women will fall at your feet for ten dollars American."

"How much for making love? I'm not into feet," said Brewster.

"Whatever you want for ten dollars, all right? But don't forget to register for the trip up the Amazon. I have written down this name of a tour guide. Use him."

"Why him?"

"Because I tell you to. He can be trusted to take your money and take you nowhere."

"I don't have to leave America for that," said Brewster.

"It is important that he take you nowhere. These things are not for you to understand. And wear this," said Francisco Braun, giving Brewster a small oblong gold bar with a bullion stamp impressed into it. "It will show your gratitude. It is a symbol I have come to love and serve. You too may be asked to serve one day for all that we have done for you."

"For what you have just done, I would wear it on my you-know-what," said Brewster.

"The chain around your neck will do," said Braun.

On the plane, comfortably seated in first class all the way to Rio, James Brewster looked at the little gold bar. It had an apothecary jar inscribed on it. With his first rum punch, he snapped the bar onto his gold chain, and rode the rest of the way to safety in absolute comfort dreaming of luxury for the rest of his life.

Consuelo Bonner did not tell Remo and Chiun how she knew James Brewster had fled to Rio. She knew and that was it.

"Policework. Straight-cut detection. You don't tell me how you know people aren't in rooms behind locked doors, and I don't tell you how I track down people."

"It would help if we knew," said Remo. "Maybe we could help you do things faster."

"Just keep me alive. That's all I want from you," said Consuelo. "If you do that, we can find out who is bribing James Brewster, and stop this uranium problem."

She noticed neither Chiun nor Remo ate on the many-hour flight to Rio. She also noticed neither of them seemed to be bothered by the oppressively hot Brazilian weather. When they were briefly out of sight, she peeked at the note she had written down back in the States when she had spoken to Braun. It had the address in Rio of a tour guide.

When they returned, Consuelo said:

"Given that a fleeing man chose a country without an extradition treaty with the United States, where would he go once he was in Brazil? Either of you two men figure that out?"

"Probably to the same sort of luxury condo he enjoyed back in the States," said Remo.

"No," said Consuelo. "The amateur mind might think that. I think he was panicked. I think I saw a frightened, terrified man back in La Jolla. I think our dispatcher who ships uranium to an accomplice and flees to Brazil keeps on fleeing. I would bet he has run up the Amazon."

"Only if you find someone who would bet with you," said Remo. "Are you sure he is in Brazil?"

"Yes," said Consuelo. She loosened the top button of her blouse. Her clothes felt like wet sacks stuck to her body. Street urchins seemed to grow out of the sidewalks. None of the travel brochures ever showed so many unwashed young people. They featured the beaches. Nor did they mention the smells of garbage. They gave you twilight photos of the city skyline. Maybe they could build high-rises in Rio but they could not collect garbage.

And the people. So many people. And it seemed that half of them were tour guides; most of them wanted to take them to nightclubs.

"We want the Amazon. We are looking for someone who has gone up the Amazon."

"To Brasilia?" asked each guide. That was the name of

the new capital that the government wanted people to
populate. There were state-paid bonuses for moving
there. Consuela was sure that there were also bonuses
for taking tourists there.

"No. Into the jungle."

"There is much jungle in Brazil. Most of it is jungle. I
have yet to have anyone ask to visit it."

"I am looking for someone who has."

"No esta here, beautiful young woman."

Consuela waited for either Remo or Chiun to say they
would never find the right guide, that the trail was lost,
that she was a fool, that she was incapable of making a
right decision because she was a woman. But by noon
when Consuelo was hot, tired, and disappointed that
neither of her companions accused her of feminine
frailty, she gave up and headed right for the name she
had taken down back in the States.

The guide was in a hotel. And he remembered a James
Brewster. The man seemed nervous. He left the day
before on a trip up the Amazon. The guide pointed to a
map of Brazil. It was like a large peculiarly shaped pear.
The green represented jungle. The dots represented
civilization. The pear had very few dots. A thin dark line
ran hundreds of miles into the green. That was the
Amazon.

"He took our main boat but we can get another," said
the guide. He spoke English. Much business was done in
English, though the main language of the country was
Portuguese.

Consuelo reserved the boat.

"Even if you find him," asked Remo, "why should he
tell you anything?"

"Because I'll promise not to follow him anymore if he
tells me who paid him. You and I are after the same
thing," she said.

"No we're not," said Remo.

"What are you after?" she asked.

"Honestly, I don't know. I just keep doing my job, and hoping someday I'll figure it out."

"I have already figured it out," said Chiun. "Your purpose in life is to make mine miserable."

"You don't have to stay. You don't have to come with me."

"It is always nice to feel welcome," said Chiun.

The Master of Sinanju did not like South America. Not only did it bear little resemblance to the modern travel brochures but it was unrecognizable from the accounts given in Chiun's histories. The Masters of Sinanju had been here before. They had served both of the great South American empires, the Mayan and Incan, and were paid well for their services. But since the Spanish and Portuguese had moved into the neighborhood, nothing was the same.

What had been great cities were now slums or areas overgrown by the jungle that had reclaimed terraces and parapets. Where gold-clad emperors had walked, monkeys now chirped in trees that grew from crevices in what had once been royal walkways.

The place, as Chiun commented on the way up to the Amazon, had become a jungle.

Consuelo, who was part Spanish, wanted to know the history of South America. Her mother's family had come from Chile.

"The tales of the Masters are only for other Masters," said Chiun.

"You should be grateful for that," said Remo.

"What can one do with a son who despises the family history?"

"Is he your son? He doesn't look Oriental," said Consuelo.

Their boat chugged through swarms of flies hovering around the mud-brown river that seemed to go on forever. The flies landed only on the guide, Consuelo, and the sailors.

Remo and Chiun seemed immune.

"He denies any possibility of Oriental blood," said Chiun. "I have to live with that."

"That's awful," said Consuelo. "You shouldn't be ashamed of what you are."

"I'm not," said Remo.

"Then why do you hide your Koreanness?" she asked. "I don't hide that I am part Hispanic. No one should be ashamed of who he is."

"He's ashamed that I'm white," said Remo, "if you want to know the truth."

"Oh," said Consuelo.

"Oh," said Remo.

"I'm sorry," said Consuelo.

The boat turned into a tributary, and the crew became nervous. The guide did not. Remo picked up little comments about something called the "Giri."

The guide said it was nothing to worry about. There were no more Giri near here. They were less than fifty miles from Rio. Would poor pitiful savages remain near Rio?

Remo checked the map. On the map, everything outlying Rio was built up but the dark green patch and the brown line they were traveling on. All it said was "Giri."

"What is Giri?" Consuelo asked a crew member when the guide had gone into the cabin to briefly escape the bugs. The Amazon and tributaries had bugs that feasted on normal insect repellent.

"Bad," said a crew member.

"What's bad about it?"

"Them," said the crew member. And then, as though even the sky might be listening, he whispered, fearful even to mention the name:

"Giri all around here. Bad. Bad." He made a motion with his hands about the size of a very large cantaloupe; then he made his hands smaller, to the size of a lemon.

"Heads. Take heads. Small."

"Headhunters. The Giri are headhunters," said Consuelo.

"Shhh," said the man. He looked to the thick foliage on the banks and crossed himself. Consuelo went directly to Remo and Chiun to warn them.

"Not Giri," said Chiun. "Anxitlgiri."

"You know them?" asked Consuelo.

"Those who know their past respect the past of others," said Chiun. The warm winds rustled his pale yellow kimono. He looked to Remo. Remo did not look back. He was watching the bugs. Any kind of bugs. Intently.

"He knows them," said Consuelo. "Will you listen to him?"

"You don't understand," said Remo. "He doesn't know them. What Sinanju remembers is who pays the bills. We probably did a hit for them, a half-dozen centuries ago or so. Don't even ask. He doesn't know."

"My own son," said Chiun.

"You poor man. What a beast he is."

"That's all right," said Chiun.

"I am sorry. I misjudged you at first because you made a sexist remark. I'm sorry. I think you are a wonderful person. And I think your son is an ingrate."

"They're still headhunters," said Remo, now looking at the riverbank. He had seen them. And they were following the boat. He was just waiting for the first arrow as Chiun described the Anxitlgiri: they were a happy people, decent, honest, and loving, with perhaps some tribal customs that would not seem familiar to whites.

Francisco Braun knew them only as Giri. He had bought heads from them before. They were dishonest and deceitful as well as vicious. But they loved gold. They loved to melt it and then pour it over favorite things, for decoration. Some of those favorite things happened to be captives whom they made slaves.

The Giri welcomed missionaries. They liked to eat their livers. A road crew, with the Brazilian army there to protect them, tried to build a highway through Giri territory. Their whitened bones ended up as hair ornaments for the Giri women.

Francisco Braun knew that one day he'd find a use for people this vicious and untrustworthy. That day in La Jolla, California, when he found that the pair could not be surprised from even a great distance out at sea, was the day he found the Giri's niche.

What Francisco knew he needed was a distraction. And the finest distraction in the world was a Giri warrior. While the pair were fighting against the poisoned arrows and spears of the Giri, Francisco would put them away.

The question was how to get two men and one woman down to a miserable patch of jungle.

The answer was James Brewster, the man he knew they would follow. And the vehicle was the woman who was chasing him, Consuelo Bonner. She trusted Francisco. And even if she did not trust, Francisco trusted the fact that her desire for him was strong enough to overcome any wariness.

That was the way he routinely made use of her kind.

Knowing they would follow, he had come down the day before and gone through the nauseating ritual of buying the Giri. The bugs had turned his fair skin into a painful red mottle. Even the repellent burned now.

Carefully he had laid out a small pile of gold at the edge of the jungle and sat down. This showed the Giri they could kill him anytime. It also indicated that the gold was a gift. If that was all there was to it, these ugly little men with haircuts like upside-down bowls would kill him as soon as eat a snack.

But Braun knew their minds. Within a half-hour the little men with their bows and arrows, wearing bones in their noses, were poking around his clearing. The first one there took the gold. The second one there took the gold from the first one. The third and fourth took it from the second. Four of them were dead and rotting in the jungle before anyone thought to speak to him.

In Portuguese, he told them there was a great deal of gold to be had. Much more than the small pile he gave them today. He said he would pay this gold for whatever they could pillage from three people who would be coming up the Giri tributary very soon. They would come on a boat. One would be a yellow man, one a white man, and one a white woman.

Who, they asked in broken Portuguese, would get the liver and the heads of the people?

He said they could keep them. He just wanted what the people had and, in exchange, he would pay ten times the amount of gold he offered as a mere gift.

Francisco knew how their minds worked. First, they would think he was an incredible fool to give up the best parts of the victims. Second, they would assume that the trio had to have much more gold with them than he was offering to pay; otherwise why would he pay it at all?

And third, they would plan to kill the three, keep the best parts, take their gold, and then collect the gold Francisco offered, as well.

For the Giri it was a foolproof scheme.

For Francisco it was a way to finally eliminate the men with the incredible powers. While a hundred men fired hundreds of little poisonous arrows, Francisco would get off three good clean shots. Then he could fly out of this armpit of the planet and return in triumph to Harrison Caldwell.

When Francisco heard the coughing engine of the river craft, he knew it would only be a few moments. The forest seemed to wriggle with the beetlelike bodies of the Giri. The whole tribe had heard of the great treasure and the good pickings that would be coming up the river. The warriors packed themselves into the slice of jungle that overlooked a narrow bend in the river. Some of the women brought pots for cooking, old iron pots taken from Portuguese traders now of course long passed through the intestines of the ancestors of the Giri.

"The Anxitlgiri are an innocent people," Chiun said as the craft chugged up the churning mud of the tributary toward a leafy point so dense with foliage no light shone through. "They do not know evil, but are susceptible to the blandishments of the more sophisticated. They served the ancient great empires as hunters and guides. What has become of them now, who knows, but they were good hunters at one time."

"Probably hunted babies," said Remo.

"Don't you ever give up?" said Consuelo.

"I've known him a bit longer than you," said Remo. "Ever heard of Ivan the Good?"

The crew did not notice the leaves in the brush, but Remo saw they did not move with the wind. They jostled in peculiar ways. Up ahead, at the point, he sensed a great mass of men. Something was going to happen. He thought of moving Consuelo behind the cabin of the river craft now, keeping her facing the farthest shore.

But Chiun refused to let him do this. Instead, the Oriental raised a single finger and ordered the boat to go directly into the shore.

"What are you doing, little father?" Remo asked in Korean.

"Shh," said Chiun.

The boat headed into the hidden mass of men. Chiun strode to the prow, letting the wind rush against his flowing yellow kimono, a small man like a flag in the front.

On shore the Giri could not believe their good luck. Sometimes riverboats got through their arrows and they would have to chase in their canoes. Sometimes they lost many men storming a boat. But this one had come ashore among them. Some of the women asked if they could start the fires now for the pots. The Giri saw the wisps of white hair floating on the breeze. They watched the beautiful pale yellow cloth billow in the wind. The men were already planning to cut it into strips for loincloths when they saw the yellow man on the prow raise his arms. And then the Giri heard a strange sound, an ancient sound, a sound they had heard spoken only around their campfires during the great ritual times.

They heard the old language of their ancestors. The small yellow man did not call them Giri, but their full proud name: Anxitlgiri. And what he was telling them in their own tongue was shame. Shame on the men and shame on the women, and shame on the children who followed.

"You move through the forests like logs, like whites.

What has happened to the hunters who served the great empires? What has happened to the Anxitlgiri men who moved like the wind kissing the forest leaf, or the women so delicate and pure they hid their faces from the sun? Where are they now? I see only clumsy stumbling fools.''

So shocked were the Anxitlgiri to hear their ritual language spoken that they rose from behind their cover. A few pots falling softly on the forest floor could be heard.

''Who are you?'' asked an elder.

''One who has memory of what the Anxitlgiri were, one who knows of your forefathers.''

''There is no need to do the hard work of our ancestors anymore. There are people to kill. Fat animals raised by the whites to steal. We need no such skills,'' said a younger hunter.

''The tales of our ancestors are but stories for children,'' said another.

In Korean, Chiun told Remo to listen to what they were saying. Remo answered: How could he, he didn't know the language—and Chiun said that if Remo had learned all the histories of the Masters he would have known Anxitlgiri.

Remo answered: The only thing he wanted to know about them was which direction was upwind.

Consuelo, fearful of all the little brown men now rising from the forests, many with human bones in their noses, asked Remo what was happening.

Remo shrugged. The boat crews shut themselves in the cabin and loaded guns. The pilot, panicked, threw the engines into reverse. Chiun told him to quiet the engines. He wanted to be heard.

He challenged the Anxitlgiri to send forward their best archer. He opened his palm.

"Come now," he said in that ancient language. "Hit this target."

And he held out his right hand, his long fingernails separating, indicating he wanted the archer to hit the center of the palm. But the archer was hungry for the gold and other things. He aimed directly at the center of the pale yellow cloth covering the man who stood on the prow, the one who had challenged the honor of the whole tribe.

The short arrow sang out from the bow. And was caught in the old man's left hand, right in front of his chest.

"How much do you miss by, little worm of a man?" Chiun asked in the old tongue of the tribe.

The archer lowered his head in shame, and put another shaft against the hide of his bow. Carefully he drew it back, and then fired at the palm. He had felled flying birds with this bow. The arrow sang out and stopped where the palm had been, clutched in the hand of the visitor.

The man had caught it. Women cried out old praises for the hunt. They banged the kettles. Youngsters cheered. Old men wept. There was pride again in the Anxitlgiri. They could hunt animals, not men. They could show pride in themselves. As one, the entire tribe began to chant the glories of the hunt.

Francisco Braun felt the vibrations of the chanting through the jungle floor as he centered his telescopic sight on the Oriental at the prow. The old face turned to the gun sight and smiled triumphantly into the cross hairs.

8

The crew remained locked in the cabin. Consuelo refused to leave the deck. Remo stood at the stern, and Chiun, triumphant, raised his arms to the multitude coming out of the jungle. One of the women brought her child that he might touch the hem of the garment of the Master of Sinanju who remembered their ancestors.

A great hunter fell to his knees and kissed the sandals beneath the pale yellow kimono.

"See how proper respect is paid," said Chiun.

"I'm not kissing your feet. C'mon. Let's get out of here."

Remo banged on the cabin. He told the crew everything was all right. But the guide refused to go on.

"I don't care how much you pay me, I'm not going on up this tributary."

"We're looking for someone," said Remo. "If he went up, we go up."

The guide took a quick peek out a window, then buried himself beneath pillows.

"No one went up. There's no point to going on."

"What about Brewster? Your company took James Brewster up the river. If he got up, we can get up."

"That's not exactly so," said the guide. "We did a bit of promotion for your trip."

"How can you promote a trip that we wanted to take in the first place?" asked Consuelo.

"We lied through our teeth," said the guide. "There never was a James Brewster."

An Anxitlgiri hunter had found a way into his cabin and was examining the guide's teeth. He took the pillow as a souvenir.

"I know there's a James Brewster," said Consuelo.

"And maybe the other guy knows there's a James Brewster, but he never took a cruise on one of our ships. We received a bonus to enhance your cultural horizon."

"Whadya mean a 'bonus to enhance our cultural horizon'?" asked Remo.

"We were bribed to steer you here."

"Who bribed you?" asked Consuelo.

"A man who wanted you to appreciate the joys of the Giri tributary. Now let's get out of here. This Indian is poking around my liver."

Chiun, hearing the conversation, called out:

"He won't harm you in my presence. He is a good man. They are all good men and women, these Anxitlgiri."

"You'd say that about anyone who would kiss your feet, little father," said Remo.

"It is not the worst form of obeisance," said Chiun, sticking out the right sandal. The left had been properly honored enough.

Remo warned the guide that the Indian standing over his cowering figure would harm him if he said so.

"Who bribed you?" asked Remo.

"I don't know his name but he had a very compelling argument for telling you that a James Brewster had gone up this tributary. He was a handsome man. Now get this Indian away, please."

"Was he blond?" asked Consuelo.

"Very," said the guide.

Consuelo turned from the cabin and dropped her head into her hands.

"I led you into this. I led you into this like a foolish girl. A trusting, foolish, lovestruck girl. I did it."

"Shhhh," said Chiun. He was about to publicly acknowledge the bowed heads of the village elders.

"He was gorgeous, Remo. The most beautiful man I have ever seen. I trusted him."

"It happens," said Remo.

"He said he was from the NCA, the agency that controls all nuclear projects and factories in the country. He had good identification. He wanted to know where you were all the time."

"I've seen him around," said Remo.

"But I saw the flight manifest. I saw Brewster's name going down to Rio. I double-checked the passport numbers. His was there. I know he went down to Rio."

"I could see him going to Rio, but not to this cesspool. Let's check Rio."

"It's such a big city. We don't know anyone."

"We can get help. You've just got to know how to be friendly," said Remo. Downriver, a bullet of a speedboat pulled away from the shore with a very blond man driving it. It kicked up a spray a full story high as it headed down the Giri tributary toward Rio. Chiun saw Remo watch the boat.

"We are not leaving yet," said Chiun. The tribal elders were preparing a dance of laudation, to be followed by odes to the greatness of the one who came in yellow robes.

"A decent people," said Chiun, "decent to those who know the histories of Sinanju."

"Decent if you like having your feet licked in a jungle," said Remo. He spoke in English now, and so did Chiun. Consuelo listened, fascinated. She couldn't miss the mass of adoring people. Who were these men? And why were they on her side?

"The histories will teach you about peoples. They will teach you who they are and who you are. The histories will teach you to survive."

Consuelo asked Remo what the histories were.

"Fairy tales," said Remo.

"I saw what happened with the Giri. They're more than fairy tales."

"The names are right. The incidents are right. But everything else is bulldocky. The good guys are the ones who pay their assassins. That's it."

"So you're assassins. Isn't that illegal?"

"Only if you're on the wrong side," said Remo.

"Who do you assassinate for?"

"You don't understand," said Remo. And he left it at that. Once again, he turned to Chiun. "Consuelo is being eaten alive out here and your foot is getting chafed. Your skin isn't used to so much adulation in one day. Let's get the show on the road."

"Exactly," said Chiun. He clapped his hands twice. "Let the laudations begin."

Harrison Caldwell had moved himself out of New York City, although the office remained there. He kept in touch every day by telephone. He had purchased two hundred and fifty acres in New Jersey, drained a swamp, planted a lawn, and had a large iron fence built around it. It was patrolled day and night by his own

guards, who wore the sign of the apothecary jar and
sword on their liveries.

He placed his own agents in charge of the bullion
office in New York City. The great talk, of course, was
why gold had not gone higher. It was the favorite metal
of international disasters. Whenever a war threatened or
broke out, whenever stocks did wild and crazy things,
people around the world invested in gold. It was the one
commodity that could be traded anywhere. Money was
paper, but gold was wealth.

And yet despite numerous small wars, numerous
warnings about the stock market, gold had remained
steady. It was as though someone was constantly feeding
in a source of gold to the international market, absorbing
any frenzy for it. There was always more gold than there
was cash and the price remained steadier than at any
time in history.

For a bullionist like the Caldwell company, the profits
should have been modest. One did not buy gold and sell
it at relatively the same price and make money. Yet
there was more money coming into the shop than at any
time in its history. More people selling for Caldwell.
More accountants. Larger bank balances around the
world. It seemed that whatever Harrison Caldwell
wanted, he could buy.

In fact, the one thing he wanted most, he could not
buy. Nor could it be rushed. There was one phone call
Harrison Caldwell wanted, but he had not gotten it.
He had told his valet that he should be awakened for
this one call. He said it would come from South America.

When it did come, Caldwell dismissed everyone. He
wanted to talk alone.

"What's wrong?" asked Caldwell.

"They are proving very resourceful."

"I have not made you my sword to find out that there is competition."

"They will be taken care of very soon."

"In the grand days of the court, there would be combat between men to decide who would be the king's champion, who would be the king's sword."

"I will take care of these two now. There is no way they are going to escape now. There will be no problem."

"We appreciate your assurances," said Caldwell, "but we cannot help but remember the grand tournaments of royal Spain. This does not mean we do not have faith in you, Francisco. This only recalls our pleasure in thinking about such tournaments. Can you imagine finding another king's champion today?"

There was silence on the other end of the phone.

"What seems to be the problem, Francisco? We know that if there is a problem with the king's sword, there soon is a problem with the king's neck."

"They are exceptional. And they will soon be exceptionally dead."

"How can you give us those assurances, since obviously you have failed at least once or twice before?"

"Because, your Majesty, they cannot escape the world they live in. I am simply going to destroy their world, and them with it."

"You please us, Francisco," said Harrison Caldwell, wondering what a destroyed world would look like. He also wondered whether he should have searched more diligently for a personal sword.

Francisco Braun's Portuguese was not as good as his Spanish but it was good enough to get just the kind of engineer he wanted. The man had a drinking problem which fortunately did not impair his competence, but most fortunately impaired his morals.

He kept looking at the diagrams and shaking his head.

"Why don't you just shoot them?" he asked after he had been paid.

"Why don't you finish the diagram of what has to be done?"

"Shooting is kinder," said the engineer. And he thought of what it would be like for those who would know they were going to die, those who would be helpless to do anything about it. He took another drink.

"Are you sure it will work?" asked Francisco.

"I'd bet my life," said the engineer, who had worked on some of the high rises on the beautiful beaches of Rio.

"You just have," said Braun.

There were problems in finding James Brewster in Rio. For one, the South American police were not that cooperative. Second, the three of them could not canvas the whole city, nor would it help them if they could: if James Brewster had stayed in Rio, no doubt, he had changed his name. Last but not least, none of them spoke Portuguese, except Chiun, who refused to help when Consuelo explained what they were looking for.

Chiun made his feelings clear in a luxury hotel room, while he prepared a scroll. It was time to record the second meeting of Sinanju and the Anxitlgiri.

"Chasing thieves is not my business," said Chiun, trying to capture exactly each syllable of the laudation odes so that future generations would know how well Sinanju had been received again in the person of Chiun.

"We may be saving the world from nuclear destruction," said Consuelo.

And with that, Chiun dismissed her from his presence.

Consuelo didn't know what she had said to offend him.

"Why should he be so angry about saving the world?"

"Because that's what I was trying to do when I should have been helping him recover the treasure of Sinanju."

"Is it that valuable?"

"Some of it was junk. But after a few thousand years you have to collect some valuable things. Gold, jewels, and the like."

"You make it sound trivial."

"If you don't spend it, what good is it? One gold bar could feed a Korean village for a century. They eat rice and fish. Sometimes duck. They like duck. But they never spent it. Look, don't worry about it. We don't need him to find Brewster."

"But you don't speak Portuguese."

"A friendly manner overcomes all barriers," said Remo.

Remo was right. You did not need a pocket translator to find a policeman who spoke English. You simply grabbed a policeman and twisted, speaking plainly and clearly in English: "Take me to your commander." There was no language barrier this simple gesture could not overcome.

Soon they were in the commander's villa. No decent police career in South America ever resulted in anything less than a villa. And no decent citizen would arrive at that villa to request justice without enough cash to pay for that justice. Remo, unfortunately, had not brought money, he explained.

The commander expressed his sorrow, but he would have to arrest Remo for assaulting the policeman he had by the neck. One didn't come down to a South American country and rough up a policeman without money in the pocket. The commander rang for the guards. Remo took their weapons and shredded them neatly onto the commander's lap. Then he showed the commander a very interesting North American message. It made the shoulder blades feel as though they were being ripped out of the body.

Its purpose was to improve his disposition.

Overcome with brotherly love, the commander pledged the honored assistance of his entire police force. Would the gringo guest please replace his shoulder blades?

"Tell your commander they are still there," Remo told the policeman who acted as translator. "They only feel as though they have been ripped out."

Remo waited for the translation. The commander asked if the honored guest could make the shoulder blades feel as though they were back in the body.

"Tell him, when we find a man named James Brewster, he will feel fine. Brewster came down here by plane a few days ago, and he probably has another name by now. We have his picture."

The search was strange from the beginning. The police force was so motivated by the sight of their bent, aching commander that it took neither threat nor reward to mobilize them. Some of the detectives commented that they had been inspired by justice, just like the American policeman "Dirty Harry."

Even stranger, when the policemen located the fugitive, after less than a day, no one handed any of them an envelope of cash.

They assumed Remo was a policeman. They asked how policemen got paid in America.

"By checks from their governments."

"Oh, we get those sometimes," said one of the detectives. "But they're too small to cash."

According to the police, James Brewster was now Arnold Diaz, alive and ensconced in one of the elegant high-rise apartment buildings facing the glorious beach of Rio de Janeiro.

Chiun, having finished recording the meeting with the Anxitlgiri, agreed to visit with Consuelo and Remo.

Downstairs, in the marble-floored lobby, Consuelo rang the buzzer for Arnold Diaz. Brewster's voice answered.

"Who is it?"

"It's us, sweetheart," said Remo.

The groan that echoed through the lobby came via the electronics from fifty stories up. The intercom suddenly switched off.

"I have a questioning technique that might be a bit more helpful with Brewster," said Remo. "I don't like guys who sell uranium on the open market."

"After what we've been through," said Consuelo. "I could almost agree with you."

"I'll be friendly," said Remo. "He'll tell us everything."

The elevator was paneled with fine wood polished to a gloss. There were even little seats. When an elevator, even a fast one, had to rise fifty stories, it took time. But the people who lived in this building weren't used to discomfort, no matter how brief.

As the elevator sped upward, Consuelo felt her ears pop as though she was taking off in an airplane. Her stomach seemed to leave her somewhere near the thirtieth floor. By the time they reached the fiftieth floor, she was dizzy and resting on one of the seats.

Remo helped her to her feet. They waited by the door. It wasn't opening. Remo looked to Chiun. A loud ugly snap of metal could be heard on both sides of the cabin. Then came a louder metallic crack and the thump of a cable falling on the elevator roof.

Consuelo felt her stomach lurch into her throat. Her body felt light, as though it were being lifted, yet her feet were still on the cabin floor. She couldn't move them. It was as though her blood had decided to flow in a new direction.

She was falling. Remo and Chiun were falling. The entire cabin was falling. The lights went out. The sound of grating, scraping metal filled the cubicle. Consuelo had to catch her breath to scream. When she shrieked into the darkness, she barely heard Remo tell her she was going to live.

She felt a strong hand on one arm and fingernails on the other. Then she felt a slight pressure. Her feet no longer touched the elevator floor. They were lifting her! And then it was as though the world had crashed. The elevator cab landed fifty stories down, shattering the cabin roof, loosening the seat, leaving them all in a dark shambles. Yet all Consuelo felt was a slight bump. Somehow these two had lifted her, and themselves, at moment of impact. It was as if they'd fallen a single foot instead of fifty stories.

Above them, as though from the tunnel of a dark universe, came a single flashlight beam. Francisco Braun shone the light from the top of the elevator shaft down into the rubble beneath him. Way down, he saw a hand reach up out of the wreckage. He saw a face. He tried to make out exactly how mangled it was.

There were the teeth. He couldn't tell that far down if they were knocked out of a mouth. But they were surrounded by lips. Definitely lips. He peered closer, straining to follow the beam to the target. He saw the lips rise on the sides. They were smiling at him. Francisco Braun dropped the light and ran.

The flashlight hit the cab as Remo and Chiun helped Consuelo out of it. She was terrified. She was furious. She checked her body. It was all there. Everything was fine, except she was going to walk the fifty stories to James Brewster's now.

"C'mon. We'll take the other elevator," said Remo.

"Are you crazy?" she asked.

"No," said Remo. "Are you?"

"We almost got killed and you want to take another elevator?"

"We showed you you wouldn't get killed even if it crashed, so why are you afraid?" asked Remo.

"I almost got killed."

"There is no almost to getting killed. You're fine. C'mon."

"I'm not going. That's it. Call me a cowardly woman. I don't care."

"Who's calling you a coward?" said Remo.

"We're calling you irrational," said Chiun. "Not cowardly."

"I'm not going," said Consuelo.

"I'll question Brewster my way, then," said Remo.

"Go ahead. Anything. Go. I am not leaving the ground. For anyone. Anything. I was almost killed. You were almost killed."

"I don't know what she is talking about," Remo said in Korean to Chiun as they entered the elevator that worked. Doormen were running over to see what was the matter. Consuelo leaned against a piece of elegant statuary to gather her composure.

Remo and Chiun pressed fifty and went up to the fiftieth floor, sure the entire world was crazy. Hadn't they shown her she didn't even need safety brakes on an elevator when she traveled with them?

"Maybe it's me, little father," said Remo. "Am I getting crazy?"

"No crazier than I," said Chiun.

"That's what I thought. 'Almost killed.' They're crazy."

James Brewster saw the bolts on the door snap off. He

watched the bar of the police lock wedged into the floor, the solid steel bar, bend backward like a safety pin as the door opened.

"Hi," said Remo. "I am being very friendly. I want to be your friend."

James Brewster wanted to be friends also. Chiun stayed in the doorway.

"Careful," said Chiun.

"Of what?" asked Remo.

"That gold is cursed," said Chiun, nodding to the pendant around Brewster's neck.

Remo looked again. The pendant seemed sort of ordinary, one of those rectangles of gold with a bullionist's mark, this one with an apothecary jar and a sword imprinted on it.

"It's just a pendant," said Remo.

"It's cursed gold. Don't touch it. If you remember the tale of Master Go . . ."

"What? C'mon. I thought you really saw something," said Remo. He walked over to James Brewster, who sat with a table between him and Remo. Brewster tried to keep that table between them, but was too slow. Remo caught up with him on his first lunge and shook hands to show friendship. Then he walked Brewster out onto the balcony and expressed his admiration of the view.

He pointed to the lovely beach fifty stories below them. He pointed with the hand that still held James Brewster. He pointed it over the balcony.

Then he explained his problem to the dangling man.

James Brewster had shipped a deadly substance around America illegally. That substance could be used to make bombs, bombs that could kill millions of people. Why would James Brewster do such an antisocial thing as that?

"I needed the money."

"Who paid you?" asked Remo.

"I don't know. The money was just deposited into my account."

"Someone must have contacted you."

"I thought it was legal."

"With nameless people depositing large sums in your account?"

"I thought I had finally struck it rich. I needed the money. Please don't drop me."

"Who ordered you to ship the uranium over strange routes?"

"It was just a voice. From the nuclear agency."

"And you didn't ask who it was?"

"He said the money took care of who he was. I needed the money."

"What for?"

"I was driving last year's car."

"Do you know how many millions of people you endangered? Do you know what one atomic bomb can do?"

"I didn't know that they were going to use the uranium for bombs."

"What else would they use stolen uranium for?"

"Maybe they wanted to start their own electrical company," said Brewster. At that moment Remo no longer wanted to be his friend and stopped shaking hands. As James Brewster left the balcony's airspace, Remo snatched the funny pendant from his neck.

Consuelo saw the body hit the place in front of the building. It landed like a water bag, with a single loud splat. Remo and Chiun arrived on the scene moments later. Remo was whistling.

"You said you were going to be friendly. You killed him for information. You killed him."

"I didn't kill him."

"What did you do, then?"

"I stopped being his friend," said Remo.

Chiun was walking several paces away from Remo. He now refused to walk near him.

"The gold is cursed," said Chiun.

Remo showed Consuelo the pendant.

"Here. See this."

"It's gold. A gold pendant," she said.

"Right," said Remo. "A silly little trinket."

"It's cursed," said Chiun.

"You will now get your first lesson in the wonderful histories of Sinanju. See for yourself how accurate they are. The Master here says this little piece of gold is cursed. Because some Master a thousand years ago said some kind of gold was cursed, the decision is written in stone. Excuse me, nice paper. No discussion. No reason. It's cursed. Period. He won't even walk near me."

Chiun refused to even look upon such disobedience. He turned away from Remo. Defiantly, Remo hung the pendant around his neck.

At the airport, Francisco Braun saw his last plan evaporate as the pair entered. If they saw him, he would never be able to place the satchel of explosives on their plane. With anyone else, hiding behind the ticket counter was good enough concealment. With these two, he doubted they would miss him. Possibly they would kill him this time. There was a limit to how many times he could miss.

They had arrived earlier than he thought, and now a mere fifty yards away the white man was walking with Consuelo Bonner. The white man couldn't miss seeing him at this distance. Braun pushed back into the corner behind the counter, waiting for the last move. Maybe he would just throw the satchel and run. Maybe he would throw the satchel at the girl, and maybe they would try to save her. Maybe he would get in a shot. All the maybes he had tried to avoid all his professional life came to him as the white and the girl came closer. And miraculously the man did not see him. No recognition. No deadly smile. Nothing.

The man went up to the ticket counter, bought three tickets for Washington, D.C., and then went to the boarding gate. He was followed at a great distance by the Oriental, who most certainly did see Francisco Braun.

The Oriental smiled slightly and waved a single finger, indicating Francisco should remove his presence. Hurriedly, Francisco left the airport, but not for good. For something seemed different to Francisco Braun. Something had changed in the white man that stirred his killer instinct. There might be a good chance now to finish at least one of them, he sensed. And if he could get one, why not two?

They had done for him what he could never have done for himself. They had split up so he could attack them one by one. And something had changed in one of them. For the first time since he had become Harrison Caldwell's sword, Francisco Braun was the one doing the smiling.

9

Chiun would not ride near Remo. He sat in the back of the plane. Remo dangled the pendant in front of Consuelo.

"Now how do you feel about the histories of the Masters of Sinanju?"

"I guess there is some nonsense associated with them. I didn't know."

"Do you think symbols can curse?" He rubbed his thumb across the apothecary jar and sword stamped into the gold.

Consuelo shook her head.

"Neither do I," said Remo. He felt the aircraft rise with too much compression for comfort. He looked back to Chiun. Chiun seemed unbothered, and simply turned his head away.

"You didn't have to pop your ears in the elevator back in Rio," said Consuelo.

"Didn't I?" asked Remo. "I don't remember." He felt tired, though it wasn't time yet for him to need sleep. Perhaps it was the steamy jungles, or the excitement at the high-rise. Perhaps it was the airplane. Perhaps it was one of those phases he had felt so often while becoming

Sinanju, one of those momentary physical relapses that came upon him like bad dreams before he took another giant step forward in achieving the sun source of all man's powers.

Then again, maybe it was the airplane food. He had eaten something he ordinarily wouldn't touch, a sort of sandwich with oils in it.

Consuelo napped as the lights dimmed. So did Remo.

When they were over the Panama Canal Zone, Remo said, "Leave it alone, little father."

And the long fingernails perched over the pendant slowly withdrew.

Francisco Braun had seen it. It was not much. But then, he did not have much. Something was different with the white and that difference might be just enough to kill him. With the team separated as they appeared to be in the airport, it could be his chance. He didn't have any others. He thought briefly about backing away from the whole thing, abandoning Harrison Caldwell.

But what were his real options? Doing hits for a few thousand dollars here and there, until one day he met with an accident? How many killers had been done in by people who gave out contracts and then didn't want to pay? How many paid as magnificently as Harrison Caldwell?

If he had only a fraction of a chance, Francisco Braun would not give up his service to Harrison Caldwell. And now he seemed not only to have that fraction but a great advantage. The advantage was that he knew where they would all have to go. The chance was what he had seen at the airport. He had seen a moment of distraction. He had glimpsed that moment when he knew he could kill a man. And, for the first time, he had seen it in the face of the white.

The Oriental, of course, had foiled the bomb attempt by noticing him. But that was all right. Alone, the old man might be easier.

And so Francisco flew back up to America with a plan, a last desperate plan that ironically might now have the best chance to work.

Knowing where they would have to go eventually, in Washington he presented himself to the director of the Nuclear Control Agency.

The first thing the man said was:

"Not here. What are you doing here? Mr. Caldwell said you would never be seen around here. Get out of here."

The portly man ran to his office door to shut it. He didn't want his secretary looking in. His name was Bennett Wilson. His flesh quivered as he spoke. His eyes were dark and pleading.

"Caldwell said you would never come here. You aren't supposed to come here. Whatever you did was supposed to be done outside the agency, so we wouldn't have to know you."

"But I am here," said Braun. "And I have bad news. A security official from the McKeesport plant is on her way to see you. Give her a day or two. She'll be here."

"Why here? Her job is in McKeesport," said Bennett Wilson.

"She seems to think someone has gotten to one of her dispatchers. She seems to think he has been taking bribes to ship uranium to strange destinations. She thinks that when she finds that person who convinced the dispatcher to send uranium to strange places, she will have solved her problem."

"That's a fraudulent lie."

"James Brewster confessed to her."

"What can he confess? He doesn't know anything.

He's just a little dispatcher who was greedy. He doesn't know who is behind it."

"He didn't have to tell them who is behind it. The people who are after you just kill their way right up the pipe until they get the man they're looking for."

"Does Caldwell know you're here?"

"I am here to take care of his enemies. Right now, his enemies are your enemies. Your enemies are his enemies." Braun's voice was smooth.

"Right. We're together. We're together in this. And we will bluff our way out. They can't do anything to us. We'll surround ourselves with memos. We'll hold meetings. We'll meet them to death. I have been working for the United States government for thirty years. I know how to stop forward progress on anything for no reason at all."

"They will kill you, I said. They are not going to try to fire you."

"That's right—they couldn't fire me. They don't have the authority."

"But they have the authority to break your bones. Or to suck the brain out of your skull. They will destroy you," said Braun. What was it, he wondered, about government officials that made them exceptionally opaque, as though the only real problem in their lives was a misplaced memo?

Bennett Wilson thought a minute. Braun had a point. Death was worse than reassignment or a departmental hearing. In those matters there was always a chance of appeal. Lately, he hadn't heard of anyone appealing a death, although there was a reference to it in the Bible. But certainly no government rule covered anything like that.

"Dead, such as the body becoming cold and buried?" asked Bennett.

"That kind of dead," said Braun.

"What are we going to do?"

"We're going to kill them first."

"I've never killed anyone," said the director of the Nuclear Control Agency. He looked back at the pictures of the electrical plans and atomic waste that decorated his office and added, "On purpose."

"You're not going to kill anyone. All I want you to do is be ready when they come here."

"After me? Are they coming after me?"

"Just lead them around in circles for a while so I can do what I have to do," said Braun.

"You mean give them partial and misleading information? Send them up, down, and around, keeping them confused with meaningless bureaucratic jargon?"

"Something like that," said Braun.

"Oh," said Wilson. "I thought you had wanted something special. If usual public policy will do, why did you come here and risk compromising me?"

"So you will have your people let me know when they arrive."

"You're not going to kill them here, are you?" Wilson held his heart. Bodies were the most difficult things to explain away in government service. They almost always required an investigation.

"No," said Braun, trying to steady the man. "I just want to watch them through monitors. I just want you to keep track of them. Nothing will happen here. And nothing will come back to you unless, of course, you create problems." And Braun explained problems would be anything that would impede his mission.

In less than a day, Consuelo and the two men registered behind the security desk of the NCA. Television monitors picked them up. Braun watched the trio from a safe room. The two men were not arguing as much but the Oriental was staying farther behind. Consuelo guided them from department to department, always putting her most adamant foot forward. "There's a cover-up going on here," said Consuelo. "I'm going to get to the bottom of it." Small chance of that, thought Braun. She hadn't even noticed the monitor. Only the Oriental seemed to give the cameras a second glance.

Braun had to admit the director was highly skilled. He did not stonewall. He did not hedge. Instead, he ordered assistance be given the security officer from McKeesport. Assistance meant four people at her beck and call, and access to all files.

For the four people she had to fill out administrative forms. And the files she got never stopped coming. The director inundated her with information.

The white male yawned. The Oriental became enraged at this. Braun, of course, did not see what Chiun saw. Nor did he understand the Korean.

"When was the last time you yawned?" asked Chiun.

"I'm not taking off the pendant," said Remo.

"It is cursed. It is killing you."

"I'm not dying," said Remo. "I am right here and very much alive."

Consuelo asked what they were arguing about. When Remo told her it was still the pendant, she told him to take it off if it bothered Chiun that much. But Remo refused. He had to live with Chiun, not her, and if he gave in now he would never hear the end of how he should live his life by the tales of the Masters of Sinanju.

The day wore on heavy for Remo. He felt the stuffiness of the room and noticed that his body was not making up for it. A fly alighted on his wrist, and he didn't notice until he saw it.

He hadn't eaten anything. He hadn't breathed

anything. And yet his body felt bloated and slow. He was skilled enough now so that he could shield it somewhat from Chiun. He knew what the old man would be looking for, jerkier movements, lack of grace, breathing that was uneven. He could fake it for a while.

He knew that his body was so well tuned it could cleanse itself of anything. And it would do so a lot better without Chiun's harangue.

Chiun kept himself farther and farther away until he did not even go into a few rooms.

A door hit Remo's shoulder.

"Excuse me," said the guard, entering the room.

"That's okay," said Remo.

That was all Francisco Braun needed to know. He had seen this man move so slowly that he was unable to avoid a door. Whatever had made that man unkillable was not with him anymore. He could kill the white now. He would not need any weapon of distance, or an elevator careening to a floor fifty stories below. He could do it with a knife.

It was dusk, and most of Washington had gone home. When Consuelo, Remo, and Chiun left the NCA headquarters on foot, the old Oriental stayed several blocks behind.

Braun stayed far from the Oriental while slowly gaining on the white. It was easy to do now. The night was warm. The white slapped mosquitoes away from his arm. Braun eased a large bowie knife of black steel out of his jacket. It was an old friend, this knife. How many times early in his life had he felt the good warm blood of his victim spurt out over the handle? How many times had he felt the target shudder? Invasion by steel was always a surprise. There was always that grunt of surprise, even when they saw it coming. As he fell in behind the white and Consuelo, he could almost taste the good feel of a blade driven into a heart. Then, when the knife almost begged for a drink of the white's blood, Francisco stepped up to an arm's length away and caught the white's neck, dragging him backward. Remo felt himself tugged back, falling to the pavement. He saw the knife coming down at his throat, but could not catch the hand. Desperately he threw an arm at the blade.

But the arm did not move fast enough. It was like a terror of a dream where some big animal was chasing him and he could not move fast enough. Nothing had felt right for days, but he knew what to do, he knew what his body should do. Unfortunately all he had were leaden legs and arms.

Still, he could sense the movements, some training that could not be lost seemed to seize him, and a dull leg moved by itself into the knife. Remo fell back, hitting his head. Dull lights flashed in front of his eyes. The knife blade was coming down again.

"It's him," screamed Consuelo, falling on the knife hand. Remo kicked again, and then, using some long-forgotten muscle strength, threw a punch. And then threw another. And another, punching into the beautiful blond face, and finally getting the knife in his own hands and ramming it right into the chest bone.

Exhausted, Remo gasped for breath on the sidewalk. Chiun finally arrived.

"Disgraceful," he said. "I never thought I would see a day when you would ball your fist and hit someone with it."

"This man attacked us."

"And he almost lived to tell about it. I am through with you, Remo, unless you remove that cursed gold."

"It's not the gold, dammit."

"You will kill yourself. The body I trained, the mind I

formed, the skills I gave will all be lost because of your stubbornness."

"Little father, I'm not feeling well. I don't know why. But one thing I do know. Your haranguing me doesn't help. Just give me a hand, help me up, and leave me alone."

"I've told you what's wrong with you," said Chiun.

"C'mon. Give me a hand."

"You must discover for yourself that I am right."

"I feel like I'm dying, and you talk about silly curses."

"Why are you dying?"

"You probably know why I feel so bad, but you just want to prove a point."

Remo shook his head. The fall had hurt.

"Give me the pendant. I could take it now, but I want you to know why you give it to me."

"I know you're busting my chops."

"Then kill yourself by ignoring the warnings of the Masters of Sinanju," said Chiun, and with a sweep of his florid kimono, turned and walked away. Consuelo helped Remo to his feet.

"He's bluffing," said Remo. "He knows what's wrong with me, but he won't tell. He's like that."

"You do seem different," said Consuelo.

"In what way?" asked Remo.

"You're not so obnoxious anymore."

"You too?" asked Remo.

"C'mon. I'll help you get well."

"Yeah," said Remo. "I feel fifteen years younger."

"I thought you said you felt awful."

"That was how I used to feel."

She put an arm around his waist and helped him off the bridge. He advised her to leave the corpse there.

"Once you get police involved, you've got problems."

"But we might be charged with murder."

"Trust me."

"I trusted him," said Consuelo. "He tried to get us killed."

"And I saved you, sweetheart. So who are you going to trust?"

"I hope you're right, Remo. But what's going to happen to the Nuclear Control Agency? We've got to report this to someone."

"I've got bad news for you," said Remo, steadying himself. "We are the someone."

"Who are you?"

"Never mind. Just take my word for it. Nothing else has worked so far."

"Why should I take your word for it?"

"Because everyone else has been trying to kill you," said Remo.

Harold W. Smith, through the organization's hidden contacts, had arranged for a special tally to be set up for calculating how much enriched uranium was being stolen. It was a rough estimate but reliable. All the enriched uranium used by legal sources was compared to all that was manufactured. The difference was how much was stolen.

The President had called this the first significant handle on the extent of the problem. But the day the President called the Folcroft Sanitarium to ask how many bombs could be made from the deficit uranium, Harold Smith gave him the most significant handle of all.

"In tonnages?"

"In how much of a city could be destroyed."

"Whoever has stolen the uranium could make enough bombs . . ." said Harold Smith, pausing to jot a few notes down on a pad, "to destroy the east coast and island as far as St. Louis."

There was a pause from the presidential end.

"Has the uranium gone overseas?"

"No indication of that, sir," said Smith.

"Then you believe it is still in the United States?"

"I believe we don't know, sir."

"So what you are telling me is that enough uranium has been stolen from us to destroy most of our major cities, and we don't have any idea what has happened to it? I mean how can they get it out of the country without setting off a million and one detectors? That's what I want to know."

"I don't think they can."

"Then the uranium is here."

"We don't know that, sir."

"What do you know? I mean, I want you to understand you are the country's last resort. What are those special two doing?"

"They are on it, sir."

"It would be nice if they got to it before half the country went up."

"They are close, I think."

"How do you know?"

"Because they have located the probable source."

"What I want to know is how uranium can be stolen from us without the Nuclear Control Agency knowing where it went."

"I think they did. They are the ones who top the suspect list so far."

"But what are they doing with it? They have all the uranium we make."

"Maybe they're selling it."

"To get us all blown up? They'll go with the rest of us."

"I don't know, sir, but I think we are quite close to finding out."

"That is the first good news I have had on this thing," said the President.

Harold W. Smith swiveled in his chair to face the lonely reaches of Long Island Sound, viewed through the one-way glass of his office.

"Yessir," he said. The President hung up. Smith looked at his watch. There had been a brief contact the day before when Remo and Chiun had returned to America. Remo had informed him of the NCA. Smith had asked if Remo wanted any backup information. Remo had answered he didn't. He felt it might only get in the way.

This, of course, meant more bodies. Smith had been almost tempted to tell him to wait for backup information. There had been so many bodies in so many places. But the figures were too ominous to ignore. All he had said was, "Fine."

And he had asked for a callback to verify success. He had given a time. He did not know where they would be. Chiun had recently taken a liking to this system. It gave him the opportunity to destroy those telephones that did not work.

According to Remo, what Chiun hated most about the telephone was the insolent servants of the wire who refused to pay him respect. He had called the American telephone system "a warren of insulting vermin." He was referring, of course, to operators.

When Smith had explained that the system used to work very well, Chiun had demanded to know what had happened.

"Someone decided to fix it," Smith had answered.

"And he was beheaded?" Chiun asked.

"No. It was a court. A court of judges that made the ruling."

"And were they beheaded?"

"No. They are judges."

"But what do you do when the judges do wrong, when they create such a dastardly warren of vermin who feel free to insult and hang up, who are rude and stupid?"

"Nothing. They are judges."

"Oh, Emperor Smith, are you not emperor or soon to be?"

This was a common question from the Oriental who never understood democracy, or laws. The House of Sinanju had only dealt with kings and tyrants before, and Chiun did not believe anything else existed.

So there was no real answer to Chiun's question that would get anyone anywhere.

"I am not. I work for the government in secret. Our President would be the closest thing to an emperor."

"Then can he behead them?"

"No. He is just the President."

"Then these judges who make the laws are accountable to no one."

"Some of them," said Smith.

"I see," Chiun had said, but later Smith had found out from Remo that Chiun had suggested both Remo and Chiun go work for the judges because they were the true emperors of the country. Remo had told him the judges were not the emperors. Chiun had asked then who did run the country, and Remo explained he wasn't sure if anyone really did.

Remo had relayed this as sort of a joke, laughing.

"It's not funny," Smith had told Remo. "I think Chiun should learn who he is working for and why."

"I've told him, Smitty, but he just won't accept it. He can't believe it isn't better to hang someone's head on a wall as an example than to go sneaking around trying not to let anyone know you exist. And sometimes, I think he's right."

"Well, I hope that your training hasn't changed you that much."

That was what Smith had told Remo. But sometimes, secretly, late at night when he, too, despaired of the country, even Harold W. Smith wondered whether Chiun was not right. He looked at his watch.

The phone rang on the second. It was Chiun. How Chiun could tell time so exactly without a watch was another mystery to Harold W. Smith.

"Oh great emperor," began Chiun, and Smith waited for the litany of praises to flow forth. Chiun would never begin a conversation without the traditional praises, which posed a problem to Smith. The director had been forced to explain to Chiun that the special scrambler lines should not be used for any great length of time. As the usage increased, so did the possibility that unscrupulous enemies could unscramble the communication. Chiun reluctantly agreed to use the short form of greetings. He could now deliver his praises in seven minutes flat.

Smith thanked him for the call and asked to speak to Remo. Chiun was never as good at relaying what was going on because no matter what was happening, according to Chiun it was happening to increase the glory of Smith.

"Remo has gone his own way. We can only feel sorry for him."

"Is he all right?"

"No."

"What's wrong?"

"He has refused to honor the memories of the Masters."

"Oh, I thought it was something serious," said Smith, relieved.

"It is a most serious matter."

"Of course. How is everything else working out?"

"There is nothing else, I must sadly say, with deep regrets."

"Yes, but how is the project?"

"Doomed," said Chiun.

"Please put Remo on."

"He is not here. I am not with him. I will not go near him."

"Yes, well, is he going to check in?"

"Who knows what disrespect he is capable of, o gracious one."

"Where can I make contact with him?"

"I can provide you with the telephone number. As you know, I am familiar now with your telephones and their mysteries."

"Good, what is the number?"

"The area code which describes the area but not the specific location of the phone begins with the illustrious number two. Then it is followed by that loveliest of numbers and the most mysterious, a zero. But lo, look again—here comes that number two again and that is the code of the area."

"So you are in Washington, D.C.," said Smith.

"Your cunning knows no bounds, gracious one," said Chiun. And he continued number by number until Smith not only had the telephone number of the motel Remo was now in but the room number as well.

He thanked Chiun and dialed. He did not like phones on switchboards but the scrambler could eliminate switchboard access to the line once he was connected to Remo. If that didn't work, Remo could always phone back.

Smith dialed, got the motel, and got the room. A woman answered.

"Is Remo there?" asked Smith.

"Who is this?"

"I'm a friend. Put him on, please."

"What's your name?"

"My name is Smith. Put him on."

"He can't come to the phone now."

"I know him personally. He can."

"No way, Mr. Smith. He's flat on his back."

"What?"

"He's flat on his back and can hardly move."

"Impossible."

"I'll bring the phone over to him. But don't talk long," said the woman.

Smith waited. He could not believe what he heard.

"Yeah," came the voice. It was Remo. But he sounded like he was suffering an incredible head cold. Remo didn't get colds. The man didn't even get tired.

"What's wrong?" asked Smith. Only his strict New England upbringing of strong reserve kept him on the operational side of panic. The phone felt moist in his hands.

"Nothing's wrong, Smitty. I'll be up in a day or two," said Remo.

10

Francisco Braun lay in the Washington, D.C. morgue for two days until a portly man with frightened brown eyes asked to see the body. He perspired profusely even though the room was cold.

When the drawer with the body was pulled out and the gray sheet folded over to reveal the pale blond hair, the man nodded.

"You know him?" asked the morgue attendant. The body still had not been identified.

"No," said the man.

"You described him pretty well."

"Yes, but it's not him."

"You sure? 'Cause we don't get too many that look like this feller. We get lots of blacks. Cut-up blacks. Burned blacks. Broke-down blacks. Blacks from the streets off the railroad tracks. Blacks with bullets in 'em. Blacks what had the bullets go right through 'em. Not too many all-white people. And this one's about as white as they come."

Bennett Wilson of the Nuclear Control Agency turned his head away, covering his nose with a handkerchief. He had not expected it to be this bad. But he had to be here. True, all he had wanted was for Braun to do his work and then get out of his life. But when he read about a blond man being found dead, he had to know it was not Braun. Because if it were, the whole thing might be unraveling, somehow. The people who might bring down Bennett Wilson's career, as Braun had threatened, might have been the ones to do the disposing. And that meant the worst of all world tragedies. Bennett Wilson might be next. And that was worth even this agony here in the morgue.

The attendant was from the Southwest. He was an old man, and Wilson was sure he took special delight in the discomfort of others. He kept on with his banter.

"Some white guys come in with cuts. Cut by blacks. Some shot by blacks. But this here a different wound. Blacks didn't do this wound."

"Excuse me, may I leave?"

"Don't ya want to give him a little pat before you go? He won't mind." The attendant laughed. He folded the sheet back.

"Know how I know this ain't a black cutting?"

Wilson thought that if he did not answer the man, the man might stop talking. He was wrong.

"Blacks slash. But this one went right into the heart. Found the opening in the ribs and *whunk*. Sent it home. I'm no cop. But I know killings. White man did this one. If a black had done it, would have been ten, fifteen cuts. Black would have cut off his dingus . . ."

All of Bennett Wilson's most recent meals came into his handkerchief as he stumbled from the morgue. He did not see the attendant hold out a hand to a fellow worker for the five-dollar payoff.

"I knew I could get that one to do a go," he said.

"I never thought he would have gone."

"You hang around the morgue long enough and keep

your eyes open, you always know. Now the real fat ones never go. Their stomachs are like iron. And the last time I saw a skinny one upchuck, I can't remember. But those fleshy ones, those just plump, are like sticking ripe plums with a shovel. Pow. Pop. Go for the hanky every time.''

Bennett Wilson threw away the handkerchief and stumbled into the sticky night air of Washington. He was not panicked enough to lose his head and roam the streets. He was just panicked enough to phone Harrison Caldwell.

He was told by Mr. Caldwell's secretary that Mr. Caldwell would be informed of the matter sometime this month.

''It's too desperate for that. I'm sure he wants to speak to me. Wilson. Bennett Wilson.''

''In what regard?''

''I can only discuss this with him personally.''

''Mr. Caldwell discusses nothing personally.''

''Well then, impersonally tell him to impersonally send someone to Washington to identify the corpse of a very blond man who knew him.''

Harrison Caldwell got the message the following day, as the butler served breakfast in a very high bed and the secretary sat at his feet. He was so stunned that he stopped calling himself ''we.''

''I don't believe it,'' he said softly.

''It's true, your Majesty,'' said the secretary.

''Yes, I suppose it is,'' said Caldwell. He dismissed the butler and secretary and climbed out of the bed, spilling grapefruit sections and the crushed ice they'd been set on onto the monogrammed sheets. The silver spoon with his apothecary monogram fell silently on the deep pile carpet. He went to the window. For miles around, all the magnificent forests were his. The guards at the gates were his. Several congressmen were his. Wilson at the NCA was his. As were some very important law-enforcement officials.

He had more gold now than England. He could buy anything in the world. And he could lose it all because of those two men.

His first instinct was to hire more bodyguards. But that would be little more than window dressing against those two. Francisco Braun, the man who had survived a challenge that had taken so many lives, the man who had been his sword, was dead. And he had been done in by two especially deadly men looking for the cause of the uranium losses to the American government. What would they do when they found Caldwell? He was sure eventually they would.

Harrison Caldwell, on that very dark morning of his life, realized he had the world at his feet except for two men who were going to take it all away from him.

At that moment, he felt he truly had become a king, because he realized that all his wealth and power had only given him the illusion of having help. He had only what he always had. Himself.

That, of course, was a great deal to have. He had the same cunning that made him the first of his family in so many centuries to reclaim what was theirs. He had the shrewdness that helped him dispose of the divers and take care of the last alchemist. There was nothing in his family history to prepare him for the complexity of his problem. But he did have one advantage: he realized how truly alone and vulnerable he was.

Harrison Caldwell refused entrance that morning to the valet, to the butler, to the personal secretary, even to some of the congressmen whom he had invited this day for a pleasant lunch among friends. He paced the room, eating nothing. But by evening he knew what he had to do. First, he had to find out who these men were. Until then he would be stumbling around like a blind man waiting for a truck to hit him. Second, he would have to find the greatest sword in the world.

And both of these things, no matter how difficult they might seem, were eminently possible because he was the richest man in the world. He had an inexhaustible supply of the one metal everyone for all time considered money.

And he had the will, the cunning, and the history to use it. He was far more dangerous than any Caldwell throughout the centuries had ever been.

He made a friendly call to Bennett Wilson in Washington.

Wilson was sure the world was after him.

"My phones may be tapped," he said.

"Do you really think we would allow such a thing to happen? Do you think we have come so long, so far, to allow something like that?" asked Caldwell. His voice was soothing, stroking, as though talking to a child.

"Come, come, our good friend, Bennett, do you think we don't know these things? Do you think we would ever endanger you?"

"He came right into my office. Right here. I saw him alive, and he assured me . . ."

"Our dear Bennett, do not trouble yourself. Come up to our place in New Jersey and ease your worries. Let me comfort you in your hour of need."

"Are we all right, we . . . I mean you and me . . . sir . . . your Highness?"

"Of course. You must come up here and let us talk. We can reassure you."

"Do you think we ought to be seen together? What with everything happening and all?"

"There is no one here to see you who does not wish to

make you comfortable. Come, let us remove the doubts and worries that plague you, good friend," said Caldwell.

Bennett Wilson heard these words while he sat in the prison of his office, terrified. On one hand there was Washington, where he jumped at every phone call, sure it would be some investigative agency that had discovered what he had done. On the other hand, there was the soothing voice of a man who said he only wanted to reassure Bennett.

Some people got their reassurance out of a bottle or a sniff of white powder. Bennett Wilson would get his from the man who had to be his friend. Why? The man was in it even deeper than Bennett. It was he who figured out everything. He who directed which dispatchers should be bribed and even selected the routes for the trucks.

Bennett Wilson was just a poor employee of the government who had made a mistake. Of course, Harrison Caldwell would protect him with all the money at the man's disposal.

Wilson was even more reassured when he saw where and how Caldwell lived. The metal fence around his estate went on for miles. Guards were at the gates. Servants groomed lawns and bushes, and carried trays around this massive brick-and-marble edifice set on a vast lawn. It was a castle. And in this castle, Harrison Caldwell was most assuredly a king.

When Bennett Wilson saw the proud figure seated on a thronelike high-backed chair, Wilson fell to his knees to kiss the offered hand.

"Your Majesty," said Bennett Wilson.

"Bennett. Our good, good Bennett," said Caldwell. "Rise. Come. Tell us your troubles."

"The man you sent is dead. I went to the morgue. Saw

him myself. They said it wasn't an accident. A professional had killed him."

"And whom did you tell about this?" asked Caldwell.

"You."

"And?"

"No one. My lord, do you think I'd want anyone else to know about these things? I never should have become involved in the first place. If it weren't for my daughter needing to go to a special college . . . I never thought I would be dealing in murder. I was just helping out an American manufacturer." Wilson was crying now.

"Bennett. Bennett. Bennett. Please. Do not trouble your heart."

"I'm so afraid," said Bennett, clutching his hands. He couldn't control his body anymore. The tears flowed freely. "They came. The ones who were at the McKeesport plant. The ones whose pictures you gave me. They came with the woman."

"What woman?"

"Director of Security Consuelo Bonner."

"And does she know?"

"No. Your man said he would take care of them. Instead, they took care of him."

"The reports implicate those two?"

"Who else could it be?"

"Many people, Bennett. Many people. Perhaps the ones you told you were coming here did it."

"I didn't tell anyone. My wife doesn't even know where I am. Do you think I would want to tell someone?"

"But certainly, you must have confided in someone. What is a world without a close friend?"

"I didn't even want to let your man into my office. But he said you sent him. Now he's dead. They killed him. They're going to get us. They will. I know it."

"What you need is some fine wine. We will pour it ourselves, with our own hands."

Harrison Caldwell led the trembling man down to the vast wine cellars of the estate. There was a special bottle there they would share, one Harrison Caldwell was saving for just such a moment, just such a friend.

"You know, Bennett, we are lonely. We know few men whom we can trust. But we know we can trust you."

"You can. All of you," said Wilson.

"But we know you must have shared these troubles, with your wife at least." Caldwell examined the bottle in the dim light. Instead of a corkscrew, Caldwell used a small thin dagger with a jeweled pommel to remove the cork. He was careful not to jiggle the dark bottle excessively. Good wine always had a sediment. If it had been served to him, it would have been allowed to rest and then been decanted, the top wine being poured into a carafe for serving into glasses. But they were just friends here in the cellar, and what was a shared bottle, somewhat murky, between friends?

"Believe me, your Majesty. I am a very secretive person. I have worked for the government all my life and I trust no one."

Caldwell passed him the bottle. Wilson shook his head. "I'm not thirsty, sir."

"Are you afraid of the wine?" asked Caldwell.

"No. No. I trust you." Bennett Wilson was almost crying again.

Caldwell gave him a warm smile, put an arm around Wilson's shoulder, and then as proof took a long mouthful of the wine. Smiling, he handed the bottle to Wilson.

Seeing Caldwell take a drink, Wilson thought it had to be safe.

"Not that I didn't trust the wine . . . or you, your Majesty. It's just that this is so dark . . . and wine cellars make me suspicious."

Caldwell said nothing, but nodded for Wilson to drink.

Wilson held the bottle in both hands and took a long hard swallow, handing the bottle back. Then he dropped the bottle. His hand didn't seem to be able to close on things too well. The crack of the bottle against the floor sounded dull and muffled. So did the sound of his head against the floor.

He wondered how he came to have such a view of the stone ceiling and why, if he had fallen, he felt no pain. His arms were there but unmovable. So were his feet. Then his Majesty Harrison Caldwell spit the mouthful of wine over Bennett Wilson's body, along with a remnant of a pill that neutralized the poison's deadly effect. Even the slight amount of absorption of liquid in the mouth could kill.

So the wine was poisoned, Wilson thought. It was a strange thought, sort of a vague far-off wondering that really didn't have much to do with anything anymore. Nothing he thought had much to do with anything. His body was numb and on its way out. And he was sure he would go with it. And then he was sure of nothing. He wasn't thinking at all.

Caldwell rubbed his tongue along his sleeve to make sure none of the poisoned wine was accidentally swallowed. He washed out his mouth and then informed the local coroner, who was on the estate's payroll, that a man had died of a heart attack in his cellar. He even spelled the words for the coroner. An inquest would not be necessary.

He even took care of the funeral, planting the portly body of the former head of the Nuclear Control Agency under the sycamore where, if the coffin rotted in time, the body might help nourish the tree.

The link between Harrison Caldwell and the uranium had now been severed. This might slow up his two enemies or even stop them completely. With no apparent leads they might never find him. He had enough gold for a while. Caldwell and Sons needed no more uranium immediately.

But he had not eliminated pathetic Wilson to sit back and live off his gold. He would finish his enemies. And with gold a man had all the power he needed if he used his mind well.

He had two things to work with. One, that Braun had failed several times to kill them, and two, that they had killed him. Therefore they were special, superior to the average hired killer.

If gold was power, knowledge was the steering wheel which guided it. And Harrison Caldwell would get just what he needed. He wanted to know everything about Braun's first failure, the failure that brought death to the Islamic Knights in McKeesport. Harrison Caldwell knew that to rewrite the history of his modern monarchy he would have to start at the very beginning.

He found out that Braun's petty criminals had had weapons which proved useless against some machine. This machine crushed bones under tremendous pressure. And yet there were no signs of any heavy machinery around the house where the bodies were found.

''You see, these guys apparently were moving toward the house. Footprints showed that,'' said the investigator Caldwell had hired to examine the killings. He was keeping a tight hand on things himself now. When it came to his life he had a very personal interest.

"Now the machine would have had to move with them because they never reached the house. But anything that powerful would have made marks in the soil itself. But it didn't. So the police there figure it was one of them."

"One of what?"

"One of the strange killings that get reported to a central office in Washington."

"So that the killer can be tracked down?" asked Caldwell. He wore a plain business suit, did not sit in a high-backed chair, and listened intently.

"I don't know," said the investigator. "Didn't seem important."

Caldwell listened to the report in full, thanked the man, and then hired someone else.

This time it was a coast-to-coast detective agency. He told them:

"There is a kind of killing that goes on in America, that the police are supposed to report to a central office. It seems as though there is a strange force loose on the land. It leaves no tracks and kills with machinelike power. Now every police department is supposed to report these kinds of killings to some central office in Washington. Don't make a big public thing of this, but find out what happens to those reports. Where they go. Who acts on them. Everything."

"Mr. Caldwell, there is no way to conduct a nationwide investigation without a tremendous amount of publicity. Can't be done. It will have to get out."

"Then just find out about McKeesport. There was a killing there recently. A half-dozen blacks. By the way, I pay for fast service."

The agency was back in a day. The situation with the reports on the special killings was this. In six places, McKeesport included, police officers reported strange sorts of killings. It was part of a national plan. They were to report to a joint committee formed by the FBI and the Secret Service.

"And that committee is where?" asked Caldwell. He had a pad in front of him.

"Glad you asked. That's the most important part of our investigation. And knowing you wanted discretion, we didn't pursue it."

"Why not?"

"Because the committee does not have an address. It is a computer terminal accessed by police departments."

"That doesn't explain why you didn't pursue it further."

"One of the killings, this one in Utah, was the brother of a motorcycle bum. He was outraged that no action was taken because everyone in his department thought the federal government would look into it. So he checked them out."

The investigator glanced down at his notes again.

"Listen to what happened. His taxes were audited and found to be lacking—by about twenty grand. His driver's license was revoked by a computer. Everything he did or tried to do involving the federal government got one cruel scrutiny, and eventually some Department of Agriculture agent got him for not reporting proper crop acreage on his family farm. It is like you touch this place and it stings. I didn't think you wanted me touching it in your name."

"You did well," said Caldwell.

"I can be of better help if you let me know as much as you can as to why. Why are you interested?"

"Good question. And I will tell you. But not today."

When the man left, Harrison Caldwell picked up the phone.

"He just left. Do you think you can clean out his office?"

"We have been at it all day."

"Good. Because now it is important."

And then, of course, he phoned the man who was watching the man he just spoke to. It struck him as a great irony that keeping his wealth safe was a lot harder than getting it.

It also struck him that he had a great natural talent for distrust and perfidy, perhaps two of the most important attributes of a monarch. You hired the bards to sing of your justice and mercy, but you kept your crown with your sword.

He would, of course, need a sword, but this one had to be superior to poor Francisco. He would also need an heir. Death was the one twist even Harrison Caldwell couldn't buy his way out of totally. But he had to postpone the death that pair and whoever sent them had planned for him. The problem was how to investigate all these killings and track down the source of that joint commission, while not becoming vulnerable himself.

To mull over that great problem, he chose a gold pool in his New Jersey estate. He soaked in the warm water and felt the gold so smooth under his feet and against his bare flesh. By midnight, he knew. He would not seek out the pair covertly. He would track them down in broad daylight. And he would make sure the world would cheer him on.

Harrison Caldwell was going to show his mercy to the world. For that one needed a bard, and the modern bard was an advertising agency.

Harrison Caldwell came to Double Image, Inc., as a philanthropist.

He had made a lot of money in his life, he said. He had

become rich beyond his wildest dreams. Now he wanted to give some of it back.

"I want to end violence in America."

Because he was one of the richest men in the world, the agency directors all thought this was seriously possible. They would have thought melting the polar ice cap for mixed drinks was seriously possible, considering this man was willing to spend thirty million in advertising.

Art directors who ate bean sprouts and communed with cosmic forces of love suddenly felt a strong urge to hang anyone committing violence.

The vice-presidents, and there were many because at ad agencies they always seemed to flourish like roaches, all agreed for the first time that violence was America's most dangerous epidemic. It needed a cure.

What Caldwell wanted was immediate advertising. He didn't want to wait a month. A week. Even days. He didn't care about the beauty of a campaign. He didn't care about artistic merit. He cared about a blitz that would begin tomorrow on radio, in newspapers, and on television, a campaign to alert Americans that they were being lied to. America was much more violent than it appeared. The country was plagued by hundreds of unsolved horrible murders. The police departments should have to account for all the deaths Americans suffered and break the conspiracy of silence.

Why, he himself knew of six deprived youngsters from Boston who were brutally slain in McKeesport, Pennsylvania. Their deaths were ignored by the police.

"I don't think we can lose our future . . ."

"Resources," suggested a copywriter.

"Yes. A wonderful word. We are endangering our future resources. We'll call them resources. How did you think up that wonderful word?"

"When you can't say anything nice about a group of people, you call them resources. What else are you going to call them, 'human disasters'? Lots of cities have directors of human resources. They are in charge of the city grief, the welfare system, the crime elements, et cetera. Resources. Or the community. You can call it the community."

"I like that word, too," said Caldwell. "We will save the community. We will save our human resources."

To save community resources, Caldwell bought a large building and staffed every office of every floor with people willing to take down as much information as callers would give. When the advertising campaign hit, an entire building proved not enough to tally the violence in America.

"Just taking down all the complaints is going to cost you a fortune, Mr. Caldwell," an adviser said.

"We must save community resources," Caldwell answered.

The Islamic Knights of Boston, heretofore a police problem, became martyrs, the Boston Six. They died, according to the newspapers, because they tried to make America a better place to live. No one bothered to interview official Islamic groups, which had never even heard of the Six.

In the flurry of advertising and publicity, Harrison Caldwell got exactly what he wanted. Extracting bits of information from the masses of useless data and hearsay, the workers in Caldwell's building put together a pattern of exceptional violence by extraordinary means. Places that had been presumed secure from any human entrance had mysteriously been entered, their occupants often killed, or threatened in such a way as to turn state's evidence and testify against even the most powerful crime lords or conspiracies.

The toughest, most ruthless hoodlums and enemy agents had been killed coast to coast by blows that could not have been delivered by humans, but only by machines. Yet mysteriously, there were no traces of machines.

Almost all of these exceptional killings had been reported to that special joint commission of the FBI and Secret Service. And none of the killers had ever been caught.

Harrison Caldwell was definitely on the trail of his enemy's home. Find out who was behind that joint commission that did nothing and he would find out, he was sure, who was behind the pair who were after him.

And for that, he needed a search through the vast maze of America's telecommunications, hundreds of detectives, computer experts, and telephone engineers. It would be the most concerted technological effort since the Space Shuttle.

It was not a major problem. All it would take would be money

Harold W. Smith saw it coming, saw the vast number of technological experts being brought from different areas, all pouring into his project searching out who received the data on the deaths, almost all of which had been done by Remo and Chiun.

Smith was not sure if it could be traced back to him. Electronics never failed to amaze him. There were machines that could tell if a person had been in a room by the amount of heat let off. Were there devices to trace who had access? He thought he had taken advanced precautions to establish blocks. But with all electronic barriers, there was always an electronic solution.

He felt very vulnerable and very alone in the office watching a giant thing out there ready to come after him.

And the Goliath behind it was Harrison Caldwell, a man not noticeably distinguished by civic virtue until this campaign. Whether Caldwell had evil purposes or not, Smith could not tell. But he had to be stopped. He had to be reasoned with. Remo could do that best.

Remo had not checked in for the last few days. On a chance, Smith reached out for him at the same motel. He was in luck. Remo was still there.

The bad news was that Remo was dead.

"What?"

"He's just stopped breathing. He didn't want a doctor. He didn't want help. He refused it, right up until the end." This from the woman who was living with him in that room.

"Does he have a pulse?"

"I don't know how to take a pulse."

"Do you have a mirror?" said Smith.

"What do you want me to do with a mirror?"

"Do you have one?"

"A pocket mirror?"

"Exactly."

"Yes. I have one in my purse."

"Take the mirror and put it to his nose and mouth."

"To see if it collects moisture. That means he's breathing."

"Yes," said Smith.

He waited in the office, drumming his fingers against the tabletop, wondering what they all had run into, wondering if what some people said about the stars were true. This was too much bad luck not to be caused by some other power.

It seemed to take forever for her to get back.

Finally she was on the phone.

"He's dead," she sobbed.

11

Smith of course was insane. Chiun had always known that but he tried to reason with him.

"Yes, you have told me that he is dead. And what can I say but that when one refuses to honor the ancestors properly, one pays the price."

"The whole organization is in trouble. You're our last resort."

"It is the lack of respect for ancestors that is the problem in the world. Respect the ancestors, and you respect what is good and decent in all civilizations."

"Can you help?"

"The power, strength, dignity, and honor of the House of Sinanju are eternally at the call of your hand, to render glory," said Chiun. Then he hung up. It was time to see Remo.

He heard the phone ringing as he prepared to leave the room he had rented but hc did not answer it. He was sure it was Smith again.

At the entrance of the hotel, one of the servants of the building beckoned Chiun. He said there was someone trying to reach him desperately.

On the chance that it was the girl Remo was staying

with, Chiun picked up the telephone. But it was Smith.

"I think we may have been cut off, and I phoned the lobby to see if you were in. They said you were on your way out. Look, we have a problem. I can't talk on this phone. Can you make a phone contact again?"

"With praise for your glory on my lips forever," said Chiun, and hung up, heading for the door.

Remo's motel was not far away. It had happened sooner than he had expected, but then Remo had advanced so much in Sinanju that it was difficult to tell where Sinanju left off and Remo began until he became insulting. Then of course, he was white.

The woman in Remo's motel room was distraught. A doctor sat by the bed. He shook his head as he removed the stethoscope from Remo's chest.

Remo lay still on the bed, his eyes shut, his chest bare, wearing only boxer shorts. His body was still. The pendant hung by the chain from his neck but now rested by his ear.

"I'm afraid it is too late," said the doctor.

"Get this white out of here," Chiun told Remo's woman, Consuelo.

"He's the doctor."

"He is not a doctor. He knows neither yin nor yang. Where are his herbs? Where is the age to show wisdom? He is only forty years old at most."

"Remo is dead," said Consuelo.

"Get him out," said Chiun. Did he have to do everything himself?

"Your friend is dead," said the doctor.

"You know nothing of death. What do you know of death? Who have you killed on purpose?"

"Well, I am going to have to file a report."

Chiun dismissed that with a hand. If the boyish doctor wished his own authorities to know how big a fool he was, this was not Chiun's problem.

When the doctor had left, Chiun told Consuelo Remo was not dead.

"Then if he is not dead, what is his problem? He sure as hell looks dead. He has no pulse. He does not breathe. The doctor says he's dead."

"His problem is stubbornness," said Chiun. He pointed to the pendant lying beside Remo's ear.

"Remove that," he said.

"What good will removing a curse do now?" asked Consuelo. It was too late. Didn't this old Oriental know that?

"Remove it," said Chiun.

"All right. It doesn't matter anymore. He was a nice guy," said Consuelo. She felt an urge to kiss Remo's forehead as a way of saying good-bye, perhaps cover him, as a fitting way to let a corpse rest. Instead she eased the chain of the pendant up over his chin and then over his head, until she had it in her hands. She offered it to the Oriental, who stepped quickly away in horror. It was faster than a step. It was a movement away to the other side of the room, and the shuffle seemed to follow him.

"Don't bring it near me. Move it away. It's cursed."

"Oh, c'mon," said Consuelo.

"Out of here. Out. Get it out."

"What am I going to do? Walk up to some stranger and say here, have a gold pendant?"

"Away."

"It must be worth several hundred dollars."

"Out of the room."

"I can't believe it," said Consuelo. "Your friend is dead and you're more worried about a piece of gold."

"Away."

"All right. I'm going. But I think you're nuts."

"The swan always looks awkward to the worm," said Chiun.

"That's insulting," said Consuelo.

"We at last can communicate, I see," said Chiun.

When Consuelo returned she saw Chiun sitting beside the bed. She could not believe what she was hearing. Here was this close friend, the one Remo had called little father, sitting on the bed hectoring Remo's corpse.

"Well, now we see. I am not one to say I told you so. But it is so. Your pride has brought you here. Your arrogance has brought you here. And why? All you had to do was listen. Listen with some respect to the House of Sinanju that has given you so much, loved you so much. But what do you do?"

Chiun paused, drawing himself up to gather more fully the greatness of the indignity he had suffered.

"Do I mind that you continued to serve the insane emperor, although truly honored positions are available in the world? No. Do I mind that when all I wanted was a little respect, that was the last thing you would give? No. Do I mind that daily, I suffered humiliations from your neglect of Sinanju? . . ."

Chiun paused a moment and thought.

"Yes, I minded it all. And here you are because of it all. How justice has finally come upon you! I told you so and you deserve it."

"How can you? That's sick," screamed Consuelo.

"And that harlot you took up with. A good Korean girl wasn't good enough for you . . ."

"Is that what you dismissed the doctor for? To lecture the body?"

Chiun cast a disdainful eye upon Remo's latest girlfriend. The boy was profligate. There was no doubt about that.

"I beg your pardon, madam," said Chiun.

"What are you doing?"

"I am talking in English because he might have momentarily lost his command of good Korean."

"I don't believe it," sobbed Consuelo. She shook her head and stumbled against a seat in the corner. "I don't believe I am hearing this."

"You of no faith. Open your eyes. Look now at the fingertips. If you cannot sense the essence of life coming back strong, then at least feel the heat."

"I don't want to touch him."

Chiun did not argue. He merely, with a deft move of his fingers to the side of her skirt, got her moving to the bed. She had to stop her hysterics.

"Touch," he said.

"I don't want to," she said.

"Touch."

She felt her hand taken by an irresistible force and laid upon the matted dark hair of Remo's chest. The body was not cold yet. She felt her hand pressed down harder. At the cup of her palm, crushing the hair into the warm flesh, she felt a delicate thump. Then another thump. Then another. The heart was beating.

"My Lord," she gasped. "You brought him back to life."

"I did not, fool. No man can do that. That even I can't do."

"But he's alive."

"He was never dead. He was indeed dying, and as he felt himself succumb he shut down his functions, so as to suffer more slowly. It was not death. It was a deep protective sleep. I am surprised he even did that adequately. He can hear everything we say. So be careful. Don't lavish him with praise. I have already spoiled him."

"I've never heard you say a nice word to him."

"I have. Many times. That is what provoked this arrogance. That is why I am ridiculed and scorned."

"When will he get better?"

"When I learn to control my nurturing instincts. Then he will listen."

Remo's eyes opened a crack, as though there were too much sun in the room. A finger stretched out, very slowly, followed by another finger, and then the whole hand opened. The chest moved gently, and Consuelo could see he was breathing.

"He is coming back," she said.

"He was never gone," said Chiun. "If he listens, he will be well in no time."

"Good," said Consuelo. "The country is in danger. We have reason to believe that those who are stealing the uranium are just those people responsible for keeping it safe. There's nowhere to turn but us."

"Your country is always in danger," Chiun told the woman. "Every time I turn around your country is in danger. We have more important things than your country. It's not the only country in the world."

Remo groaned.

"Quiet," said Chiun. "It is your time to listen. If you had listened before with respect, you would not be here, disgracefully on your back in a motel room with a strange woman."

"You mean you're not going to help. Whatever he has sufferred he has suffered in the line of duty," said Consuelo.

"No, he hasn't. He's been punished for disrespect. What is this line of duty, and suffering? You are not supposed to suffer if you are an assassin. The other person is supposed to suffer," said Chiun.

"So you are not going to help America?"

Chiun looked at the woman as though she were mad. There were things Remo had to understand. He had to know why the gold was cursed. He had to know the tales of Master Go and why removing the pendant took away the curse from his body. He had to think correctly again.

"Then you will not help either?"

"I am helping. I am helping whom I should help."

"Do you know that the uranium stolen could blow up thousands and thousands of people with horrible bombs?"

"I didn't make the bombs," said Chiun. What was this woman talking about?

"But you can stop them being made."

"By whom?" said Chiun. He saw Remo regain functions in the fingertips and the function control move up the arms. He massaged the shoulders. He lifted Remo's lips and examined the gums. Good. Good color. It had not gone too far.

"We don't know," said Consuelo.

"Then why should I attack someone whom I don't even know? The violence in this country is awful. I have seen it on your television. I know your country. Random violence among strangers, and not one professional assassination in how many Presidents who have been killed? I know your country, young woman," said Chiun. He opened Remo's eyelids wider to see the whites. Good. The pupils were coming back too.

"Please," said Consuelo. "Remo would want you to help his country."

"Just a minute," said Chiun, turning to the pleading woman.

"President McKinley. Assassinated. Amateur. John F. Kennedy. Dead. Another amateur. No payment involved anywhere. Your President Reagan missed on a city street by a mind-troubled boy. Another amateur. And this is a country you wish a professional assassin to save? You are not worth saving."

"Remo. Talk to him, please," said Consuelo.

But Remo did not answer.

"I'll do it myself then. Remo, if you can hear me, remember I am going to NCA headquarters. I believe what you said. I believe we're the only ones who can save the country. I want you to carry on if I don't come back. I know you love America too. I guess I was always ambitious to prove I was as good as any man. But right now, all I want to do is save our country."

"Are you through?" said Chiun.

"Yes," said Consuelo. There were tears in her eyes now and she was not ashamed of them.

"Then close the door behind you, thank you," said Chiun.

"If Remo didn't hear me, and he comes to, would you tell him what I said?"

"Of course not," said Chiun.

"And I used to think you were the nice one," said Consuelo.

"And you were correct, too," said Chiun.

"You're horrible, you know. Really horrible. Remo was right."

"Did he say that?"

"He said you were difficult."

Chiun smiled. "I can't believe that," he said. His trainer had been difficult. His grandfather had been difficult. But the one thing about Chiun that Chiun understood above all things was that he was not difficult. If he had a problem, it was his tendency to be too nice. That was Chiun's problem. That was where all the trouble came from.

Chiun felt her turn on her heel and walk out the door. He examined the chest, the legs, the ears, all the meridians of the body. Good. Not much damage. The unity of the body, the rhythms, were off. But they would come back. He would be the same again, but this time Remo would meet a different Chiun. No more Mr. Nice Guy. No more being pushed around. He was through taking it anymore.

Since it was midday, he turned on the television. Ordinarily he did not watch advertisements between the daytime dramas. But this day he saw an advertisement that moved him. Someone had finally woken up to the trouble America was in.

An American businessman was addressing the nation. He called for an end to random violence. He called upon America to make its streets safe. He called upon every citizen to report horrendous acts of unpunished crimes to his clearinghouse. The man had a proud high-bridged Spanish face. He spoke with haughty grandeur. There was something nice about the man.

With an American writing implement of crude blue ink, Chiun sat down to write a letter to this man on motel stationery. It began:

Mr Dear Mr. Harrison Caldwell:
    You have finally come to save this wretched

country from its excesses. Too long has America
suffered from the amateur assassin violating the
standards of the noblest profession, throwing the
streets into chaos . . .

If Consuelo Bonner had any thought about trying to
get help, she gave it up as soon as she checked with her
McKeesport plant.

"Better not come back here, Ms. Bonner," said her
secretary. "They're looking for you."

"Who?"

"Everyone. Police, federal authorities, NCA. You're
listed as a fugitive."

"I wasn't running from anything, I was chasing
something."

"I told them, Ms. Bonner. I told them you were the
best security chief this plant ever had. I told them you
were better than any man. All they said was that I had to
let them know if I heard from you. Or I'd face federal
charges."

"I'll get this straightened out myself. I just need my
records."

"We don't have them anymore. All the files were
seized. They're evidence."

"I see," said Consuelo.

She could turn herself in and explain everything. But
would they believe her? Only if she had the files she had
left at headquarters, the ones leading to the man who
contacted James Brewster. Maybe Brewster didn't know
who had reached out for him, but there couldn't be too
many people at headquarters who knew a lowly
dispatcher outside of the plant.

She would have to break in herself. If she had Remo,

he could get in any number of ways. The man could probably break through a wall when he was well.

She had one thing going for her. She was one of the security people who set up the original procedures to protect vital NCA files. She knew what guards would look for and what they would not look for. Such as a clearance badge. They never cross-checked the names, or even compared faces. What they did look for was the number.

Consuelo Bonner carefully cut her badge out of its laminated container, painted in new numbers that looked original, gave herself the name Barbara Gleason, and then resealed it all. Then, at midday, she marched into the vast concrete buildings of NCA as though she belonged there.

Expecting to be arrested any moment, she was almost horrified at how easy it was to get into the records center.

After a short time in front of a microfilm machine she nearly forgot there was any danger at all.

She got Brewster's file easily, saw his date of employment, his early retirement. She even saw some of her queries about him. She had sought background checks on everyone who had anything to do with the missing uranium. But on Brewster, the queries just sat in the file. A note was attached to them. If was dated the moment they came in. The memo said: ''Brewster okay.''

It seemed to have the highest authority. She checked out the authorization code. When she saw who it was, she couldn't believe it. It was Bennett Wilson himself. The director of the whole shebang.

He was the man she was intending to report to when she unraveled everything.

She closed the file. A guard was looking at her. Something puzzled him about her. She had seen him a few days before when she was here with Remo and Chiun.

She pretended she was busy in the file. She reread Brewster's early application for government employment as though it were a best-selling novel.

What did Brewster want to do with his life?

"Retire," was his answer.

If Brewster saw a mother and child drowning and he still had an envelope to lick for a magazine subscription, would he:

A. Save the mother and child, forgetting about everything else?

B. Put down the letter and then save the mother and child, leaving the letter for later? or

C. Make sure he had the correct postage and leave the fate of the mother and child to those who might be qualified to help?

Brewster chose C.

Consuelo glanced up. The guard was still looking. She went back to Brewster's entrance test.

The next question was another multiple choice. Which of the following would he prefer to watch?

A. The last minutes of a Super Bowl game tied 48 to 48.

B. *Swan Lake* performed by the Royal Ballet.

C. Rembrandt at work.

D. The clock.

Brewster had chosen D, for one of the highest scores ever recorded for a federal job, so high the examiner said that if there was a person born for government service, it was James Brewster.

"You."

It was the guard. Consuelo looked up.

"Yes?" said Consuelo.

"Let me see your identification badge."

Consuelo handed it to him, making sure the ends of the laminate she had just glued got one last pressing together.

"Didn't I see you here the other day?"

"You may have, I don't know."

"I have a photographic memory."

"Then you must have."

"You weren't named Barbara Gleason then. Consuelo Bonner? Right. Consuelo Bonner, McKeesport security. Right? Right?"

Consuelo swallowed.

"Right," she said. It was all over.

"I knew it. I have a photographic memory."

"What are you going to do?" said Consuelo. It was over. Having been caught, her accusations now would only look like trying to protect herself.

"What do you mean, what am I going to do?"

"You've found me with questionable identification."

"Right. But this ain't my floor. I just came here to get a look at my own file. I legally have a half day's vacation due from my 87-35 revolving vacation leave, 803967 transfer code."

"So you are going to do nothing."

"This is the last part of my lunch hour. I am not going to cut into my lunch hour for this. I don't know that I'd get it back. Could you guarantee me compensatory time for my lunch break?"

"No," said Consuelo.

"Then forget it. I just wanted to see if I was right."

Almost sadly she returned the folder to the file she had gotten it from. She hated the idea that it could be so easy to break in here, even if she had done the break-ing. She had tried to change things at the McKeesport plant and felt to a large degree that she had succeeded, except for the thefts. But what could she have done when they were masterminded by the very head of the agency?

As she was about to leave, she saw an "all-staff memo" posted on a wall. It was from the new chairman of the NCA. It was a notice of regrets for absence of Director Bennett Wilson, and assuring everyone NCA would run even better while they looked for his replacement. Until then the chairman would personally run everything.

But it also added that things would now be changed. Too many employees were just waiting around until retirement. Too many ignored their duty because they felt their jobs were guaranteed safe. Well, said the new chairman of NCA, he was going to appoint someone soon who felt nuclear materials were too important for a nine-to-five attitude. Heads were going to roll. People were going to do more than what they could be blamed for or he personally would shut down the entire system himself and start from scratch.

The warning was that the job endangered was yours. And until he got a replacement for Wilson who felt the same way, he would run things himself.

Salvation, thought Consuelo. Barely able to control her excitement, she hastily scribbled the notes on Brewster and Wilson. This was what she had hoped would always happen to the NCA. It had seemed as though there was so much protection for the comfortable jobs of employ-ees, none was left over for the uranium.

This man was going to change it. This man would

listen to her. This man would make sure they would track down whoever was working with the director. She was sure there were other Brewsters in the system. They would account for the massive amounts of missing fissionable material.

She had broken the case and the new chairman would do the mopping-up. The guard cut into his lunch hour to tell her that the new chairman never came to the building itself, but worked from his home in a nearby state. Since it was only two hours' drive from Washington, Consuelo Bonner rented a car. She just knew that this sort of person would drop everything to hear her information. She headed north into New Jersey.

He lived on an estate that appeared well-guarded. No little phony badge would get her through these people, she knew. She explained who she was and why she was there. She guaranteed to the guard that if they got her message through, he would see her. The guard wasn't sure.

"I know that when he finds out what I have, he will be grateful to you. Tell him that I am a security officer from one of the nuclear facilities in America and I have evidence with me now that Bennett Wilson, the late director, was involved in a scheme to steal uranium. I know because one of my dispatchers was helping him do it."

The guard hesitated.

"Look, my name is Consuelo Bonner and the police are looking for me and I wouldn't be here risking myself if I didn't have the goods."

"Well . . ." said the guard. He wasn't sure. Finally he shrugged and phoned the main house. He went through four people, each more important than the last. Consuelo knew this because the guard's body became more rigid with each person he spoke to. When he hung up the phone he was shaking his head.

"You're right. I never thought he would see you. But he'll see you right now. Just drive right in, and go to the biggest house you'll see and ask. Someone will take you to him immediately. Mr. Harrison Caldwell wants to see you right away."

Mr. Caldwell seemed like an odd choice for the chairman of such an agency. Recently very wealthy, he had donated grand sums to all political parties, and could have had the best ambassadorship at the disposal of any president. But as he explained it to Consuelo, he wanted to help America. Give something back for what he'd taken.

He had grand haughty features, dark eyes peering over a proud nose. He sat erect in a high-backed chair, in a velvet robe bordered thickly with gold lace.

He drank a dark liquid from a goblet and did not seem to feel obliged to offer Consuelo anything, although she mentioned she was very thirsty. Caldwell said that would be taken care of later.

"That's all I know now," said Consuelo. "But I am sure if we pursue this, we will find others. Lots of uranium has been stolen. And this explains why this man who tried to kill my friends got clearance so easily. The man was obviously a killer, and yet he had a security clearance from NCA. His name was Francisco Braun."

"And what happened to him?"

"Well, I guess it has to come out sooner or later, and we were defending ourselves. We did him in."

"We? Then you worked with another ally of good government. Good," said Caldwell. "We should help him. We should thank him. That's the sort of man we need. Where can we reach him?"

"Well, it is a him," said Consuelo. "But there were two. Both men."

"You are insulted that I assume they were men."

"Well . . . yes. I was. They could have been women. Although I've never seen men like them."

"Yes, well, we have to get them on our side, don't we?" said Caldwell. "We'll take them away from whoever they're working for."

"I don't know who they're working for. The white guy, Remo, just calls himself one of the good guys. He's getting better now, I hope."

"From his fight with this man Braun?"

"No. Some form of old curse."

"You have done well for us, Ms. Bonner. We are pleased. 'Consuelo' is Spanish. Do you have any Spanish ancestry?"

"My mother's side. Castilian."

"Any noble blood?"

"Only if someone got out on the wrong side of the mattress. Illegitimate noble blood possibly."

"We can tell, you know," said Caldwell.

"The Nuclear Control Agency?"

"No," said Caldwell, pointing to himself. "Well, thank you very much for your time. Now you may leave."

"You are going to do something about this?" asked Consuelo.

"You can be sure of it," said Harrison Caldwell.

Consuelo was taken from the immense gilded room, through an exquisite hallway bordered by massive paintings and statues. Gilt seemed to be everywhere. She saw one banner thirty feet high embroidered with what seemed to be a gold coat of arms against a purple velvet background.

She had seen that coat of arms before but couldn't place it. Only when they locked the iron bars behind her did she remember it. It was the apothecary jar on Remo's pendant.

The bars did not open. The room was dark and had a single cot. The walls were stone. There were other small rooms with bars. It wasn't exactly a jail. It was too dank for that. She was in a dungeon. And then the bodies started being brought down. All she could make out was that there was some kind of contest upstairs somewhere where people were killing themselves to see who was the toughest.

Out on Long Island Sound a boat stopped, and several men with binoculars pointed to a large brick-enclosed institution. It was Folcroft Sanitarium.

"Is that it?" asked one. He was loading a clip in a small submachine gun.

"That has to be it. No confluence of electronic signals could come from anywhere else," said the engineer.

"All right," said the man with the submachine gun. "Tell Mr. Caldwell we found his target."

On one high corner of the building was a room with mirrors reflecting outside. Inside was Harold W. Smith, and he did not know whether he was lucky or unlucky.

Folcroft's defense systems could read anything sending and receiving signals within a radius of twenty miles. And when he had focused it on that suspicious boat out in the sound, he read that someone had found him and was told to wait until reinforcements arrived so they could surround the sanitarium and make sure no one got away.

12

Remo could see the room, feel the bed, feel his arms, and most important, breathe properly, breathe to get his balance, his center, and himself. But his head was still ringing when Chiun told him for the seventeenth time, he was not going to say he told him so.

"Say it. Say it and get it over with. My head feels like it was sandpapered from the inside."

"No," said Chiun. "The wise teacher knows when the pupil understands."

"Tell me it was the curse of the gold that did it to me, and then leave me alone," said Remo.

"Never," said Chiun.

"Okay, then don't tell me you're not going to tell me again. I don't want to hear it."

"All right, I'll tell you. I told you so," said Chiun. "But would you listen? No. You never listen. I told you the gold was cursed. But no, you don't believe in curses even when their secrets are chronicled in the glorious past of Sinanju."

"You mean Master Go and the Spanish gold?"

"No. Master Go and the cursed gold."

"I remember it. Master Go. Somebody paid with the

bad check for the day—rotten gold—and he refused to take it. That was around six hundred years ago. Maybe three hundred. Somewhere in there. Can I get a glass of water?''

''I will get it for you. If you had listened to me about the cursed gold at the beginning, then you would be able to get it yourself.''

''You said you weren't going to mention it.''

''I didn't. I said I was getting you water. But it would not hurt for you to recite Master Go again.''

''Not now. The last thing I want to hear now is a recitation of the Masters.''

''Just Go.''

''But even the Lesser Wang would be too much,'' said Remo, who knew that the entire history of the Lesser Wang was exactly two sentences, while the Great Wang took a day and a half if you rushed. Wang the Lesser was a Master of Sinanju during an odd period of history when peace settled over most of the world. This era was called the unfortunate confluence of the stars. Since there seemed to be a minimum of strife among rulers, the Lesser Wang spent most of his life sitting in Sinanju waiting for an overthrow, an attack, or a decent usurper to come along. When he finally got one request for service, it turned out not to be worth even leaving the village for. As a result, the tales of the Lesser Wang went like this: ''Wang was. And he didn't.'' It was the only brief thing Remo had ever heard Chiun recite. But even that seemed overwhelming to Remo.

''Then I will do it,'' said Chiun, ''because you should know why you suffered.''

And thus Chiun began the tale of Master Go, who had gone west to the many kingdoms of Spain in the year of the duck, and in a time of modest prosperity for the

House of Sinanju. There was good work in most of
Europe because of an outbreak of civil wars, but Master
Go chose the somewhat peaceful Spanish king because
of a most interesting situation. The king said he wanted
the Master of Sinanju to kill enemies he had yet to make.

Now Master Go thought this might be a new, more
intelligent way to use an assassin. Why, he asked
himself, should kings wait until they made enemies
before calling on an assassin? Why not prepare
beforehand? It could only bring honor and glory to
Sinanju to serve such a wise king.

But when he reached the court of the Spanish king and
enjoyed an audience, he found out the king had no
specific enemy in mind.

"Everyone will be my enemy who is not my friend,
and even some of my friends will become enemies."

"And how is that, your Majesty?" asked Master Go in
the formal manner of the Spanish court.

"I am to be the wealthiest man in the world," said the
king.

Now Master Go said nothing. Many of the Western
kings, like little children, considered only their small
place and time in the world. Though these kings were
the richest of their regions, there were many wealthy
kings elsewhere whom Westerners had never heard of,
with jewels and gold that would make even the richest
in the West seem poor. But, as is proper, Master Go said
nothing, for an emperor's enemies, not his ignorance,
are what a Master of Sinanju comes to cure.

"I have more than a gold mine. I have the mine of the
human mind."

With that, the king ordered many weights of lead to be
brought to him, and he called his alchemist before him
and said, "Show this man from the Orient how you can
change lead into gold."

Now the alchemist, rightly fearing disclosure of his secret, performed his transformations in private. But though there are defenses against most men, the defenses against Sinanju are none. The Master easily made himself into the silent shadow of the alchemist to watch and see if the man indeed could make gold from lead.

And he did, mixing the lead with many ingredients. But he also added real gold, the gold paid by the Spanish king. And all of this, he claimed, he made from lead. What this meant, Master Go did not know, until he saw the alchemist receive more money to make more gold for the king. Money was, of course, gold. And this time, the alchemist added even more of the king's gold to the pile he claimed he produced.

And again the alchemist received gold, and again he gave back more until finally the king emptied his treasury. With all that money the alchemist and an evil minister began to purchase something more valuable than any treasure—the loyalties of the army—and this time did not return any gold to the king.

But before the minister and alchemist could seize the crown, Master Go went to the king and told him of the plan. The alchemist fled with only a small portion of the gold and his secret. In gratitude, the king paid Go with some of the gold made by the evil alchemist.

But Master Go refused it.

"Your Majesty, this gold may be good for you, but for us it is cursed. I have seen the ingredients used, and in them is something that makes a fully trained body nauseous in its most essential humors."

"Do you mean, great Master of Sinanju who has saved the crown of Aragon and Asturias, who has brought the wisdom of your magnificence here before us, that this gold is not good?"

"No, your Majesty. The gold is good because it can buy things, it can coat things, it can be used for ornament and tool, but for us, it is cursed."

And the king gave Master Go good gold, none of it marked with the curse of the evil alchemist, the stamp of the apothecary jar.

This then, centuries later, was noticed by Master Chiun but ignored by the impetuous, disrespectful Remo. And thus did the stubborn Remo bring harm to his body because he heeded the influence of bad white habits instead of the glory of Sinanju.

"You added to an old legend, little father," said Remo. By the time Chiun had finished repeating the tale he was sitting up. He felt as though the retelling had put carbonated water in his bloodstream. "I thought the legends were eternal. You can't rewrite them."

"I added nothing to history but history. Didn't you feel anything when you held the pendant close to you?"

"I was angry at being bugged."

"Any silliness like anger diminishes the senses. Lust diminishes the senses. Greed diminishes the senses. The stronger the emotion, the less we perceive," said Chiun.

"You get angry. You get angry all the time."

"I never get angry," said Chiun. "And to be accused of such makes my blood boil."

"When will I get better?"

"You'll never get better. You're an evil child, Remo. I've got to face that."

"I mean physically. When will I recover from this thing that hit me?"

"Your body will tell you."

"You're right," said Remo. "I should have known." He finished the water, easing himself out of the bed. It felt good to move again, although he had to think about every step.

"What was in that stuff the alchemist used? How did Master Go know there was poison in it?"

"Doesn't your body know poison? Did you have to wear a badge like the others at the manufacturing plant in McKeesport? Do you have to see whether it changes colors to know if you are receiving harmful essences through the air?"

"Radiation. Uranium. He made the gold with uranium. Do you think the uranium being stolen now is going not to make bombs but to make gold? Do you think someone has rediscovered that old formula?"

"No," said Chiun.

"Why not?" asked Remo.

"Because I don't think about things that are so trivial. Remo, I have saved your life again. Not that I am bringing it up. But I have. And for what? For you to care about these foolish things? Are we guards of metals? Are we mere slaves? What have I given you Sinanju for but to enhance your glory and that of the House of Sinanju, and here we are with puzzles. Do I think this? Do I think that? I will tell you what I think. I think we should leave mad Emperor Smith, who will never seize the throne. We should serve a real king."

Remo made his way to the bathroom and washed his face. He had heard this a lot. He would hear it more often now that he had almost gotten himself killed.

The phone rang. Chiun answered it. Remo could tell it was Smith. There were the flowery protestations of loyalty, the grandiose exaltations of Smith's wisdom, and then the hanging-up with a flourish of the hand, like a rose being brought ceremonially to its rest in a gilded vase. But this time, Chiun had said something strange.

"We shall hang their heads from the Folcroft walls, and speak their pain as your glory forever," Chiun had said to Smith.

"What's happening, little father?" asked Remo.

"Nothing," said Chiun. "Don't forget to wash your nostrils. You breathe through them."

"I always wash my nostrils. Who are the people we're supposed to do in?"

"Nobody."

"But you said we'd hang heads on walls. Whose heads?"

"I don't know what Smith talks about. He's mad."

"Who?"

"No one. Some people who have surrounded the fortress he calls a sanitarium. Now don't forget your nostrils."

"They have Folcroft surrounded? The whole thing can go under."

"There are other lunatics if you prefer."

Remo moved to the phone. His legs were not quite working right and he had to force them ahead in a crude sort of walk, something he had not done since before training. He got the motel switchboard and had them place a call. He didn't know if the security codes would work on this open line, but if they took Smith and Folcroft, everything else was over anyway.

Smith answered right away.

"Open line," said Remo.

"Doesn't matter. They're closing in."

"How much time?"

"Don't know. They're holding off until they can make sure I won't be able to get out. I am going to have to go into a destruct as soon as that happens, you know. In that case we won't be seeing each other, and you can terminate your service."

"Don't give up yet, Smitty. Don't take that pill I know you have with you."

"I'll have to. I can't be taken. The whole country will be compromised."

"Just hold on. I'm coming up. There's a small airport in Rye, isn't there?"

"Yes. Right near here."

"Use those magnificent computers and get me clearance on some plane that will get me up there fast. Hold on. I'm coming."

"How are you? I thought you were dead."

"Get me the plane," said Remo. He only had to wait thirty seconds before Smith had gotten him a clearance on a private government jet out of Dulles Airport.

"Where are you going?" said Chiun. "You were lying in bed helpless moments ago."

"I'm helping Smitty. And you should too. You always tell me how Sinanju has never lost an emperor. Well, he's an emperor."

"No, he is not. He is the appointed head of CURE, an organization set up to protect your country by doing things the government wouldn't dare get caught doing."

"So you do know," yelled Remo. "So you do understand. What was going on all those years with the Emperor Smith business?"

Remo found his slacks and shoes and put them on, and walked to the door.

"He's not an emperor. And besides, it is his wish to die and release you. I couldn't help overhearing what he said."

"Especially since your ear was next to mine."

"You can't go there in that condition. You're no better than a normal human being. Maybe one of their prizefighters. You could get killed."

"I'm going."

"Then I must go with you. With luck Smith will kill

himself and then we can all leave, as he suggested. He did say it. Those were his words. One must obey."

"Now, one must obey," said Remo angrily.

In the cab on the way to the airport, Chiun reminded Remo how to breathe and massaged his lungs through his back. The cabbie wondered what they were doing back there. Obviously the younger man was sick. He offered to help Remo out of the back seat, hoping for a larger tip. His response was obliterated by the scream of the jet engines. The cabdriver covered his ears. So did Remo. Chiun of course could equalize the pressure within his head, as Remo used to be able to do. Chiun shook his head.

"I'll go and save mad Smith, and you stay here."

"No. I'm going. Somehow I feel he may find himself unsaved if you go alone."

On the plane they sat behind the pilot. Chiun suggested they might want to see the coast of Florida before they went to Rye, New York.

They landed within an hour. Remo grabbed another cab. Chiun joined him, making sure the driver idled his motor a few moments because, as Chiun said, he did not want Remo breathing fumes from unidled motors.

"Never mind him. Get going," said Remo.

"How much do you charge per meter travel?"

"It's a regular fare to the sanitarium."

"I never pay regular fares. They are unreliable," said Chiun.

"Don't worry. He'll pay. Get going," said Remo.

"He said he wouldn't."

"I'll pay," said Remo. And to Chiun: "You never give up, do you?"

Chiun raised his hands in a motion of the supplication of the innocent. His eyes widened in curiosity, as if the very suggestion of deviousness lacerated his purest of souls.

"If Emperor Smith is dead by the time we get there, it is not our fault."

"No, but it's your hope," said Remo.

"Is it a sin to want only the best for you and your skills? Is it a crime?"

Remo didn't answer. He forced his breathing. Somehow the more he breathed, the more harm that had been caused by the uranium-tainted gold eased out of his body. He practiced short finger moves, positions of his body. To the cabdriver, the passenger looked vaguely as though he itched. Remo was getting ready.

At the high brick walls of Folcroft Sanitarium, Remo saw the problem instantly. Two boats were bobbing in the sound, holding a position. They did not move with the other boat traffic but appeared to have anchored to fish where no one else was fishing. Large tractor trailers blocked both entrances to the building and men dressed as movers waited in the backs of the open vans. If they had carried screwdrivers they would have moved with lightness. But they didn't. They all moved as though they had weapons; their steps were the movements of men who maneuvered around their pieces instead of with them. No one, no matter how experienced with arms, ever moved as though the weapon was not there. Remo had not believed it in his early training; he had tested Chiun's ability to detect a concealed weapon again and again. He could have sworn that when he was just a policeman, before he was trained, he himself was seldom conscious of the gun he carried. But Chiun had said that he had always known it was there even if his mind didn't.

Remo didn't understand what Chiun was talk-

ing about until he had actually seen it in action,
when he knew someone was carrying a weapon
by the way the body moved, even when the person had become so used to it he forgot it was
there.

Now Remo left the cab. The problem was how could
he do what he knew he had to do with what he had left.
He looked up to the high corner mirror windows. He
hoped Smith had seen him, hoped he had not taken that
pill to remove himself and the danger of exposing the
organization.

He waved but did not know if there was anyone up
there alive to wave back.

"You're going to die," said Chiun. "You're not
ready."

"There are some things worth dying for, Chiun."

"What idiot whiteness is that? Did I train you to get
killed like some white hero, like some kamikaze
Japanese? There is nothing worth dying for. Who tells
you this craziness?"

Chiun got out of the cab too. The driver wanted to be
paid. This in itself was a task, because Chiun did not
surrender money lightly. He did not believe in paying.
He pulled a silk coin purse from the sleeve of his
kimono. When he opened it, dust rose from its folds.

"That's it?" said the driver.

"To the penny," said Chiun. Chiun also did not
believe in tipping.

Four large men, dressed as movers, ambled over to
Remo.

"We're moving this place today, buddy. You got to get
out of here."

"Wait a minute," said Remo.

"There's no waiting. You gotta get out of here."

"Have you paid?" said Remo, turning to Chiun. He

felt one of the men try to lift him. He wasn't sure what the best response was, actually how much he had to work with. So he pretended the man's arm was actually a much stronger steel beam. He needn't have. The large arm went sailing down the road like a forward pass. He had enough control.

"Stop that," screamed Chiun. "Smith will see your balance. You're not ready to fight. Your rhythms are wrong. Your breathing is wrong."

With a single blow into the chest, Remo dropped the man who had lost the arm, stopping his heart. Then he felled the other one by collapsing the spine with a blow through the belly. The man folded like a card table. A pistol dropped out of his shirt. The cabdriver suddenly decided he did not really need a tip, dived into his car, and had the accelerator to the floor before he got his hands fully on the steering wheel.

The trucks began emptying and the guns came out, some automatics, some rifles, some pistols.

"Quick. Hide," said Chiun.

"From what?"

"From showing how badly you work. You are disgracing the House of Sinanju."

"I'm good enough."

"Good enough is not Sinanju."

"You mean to tell me you think Smith can tell the difference between balanced breathing and internal rhythms? He doesn't even know one blow from another."

"You never know what an emperor knows."

"Since when is he an emperor again?" said Remo.

"Since he may be watching," said Chiun. "Sit, and watch perfection."

There wasn't that much to watch, since Chiun made short work of the attackers, but the Master did show off some variations for Remo. But each variation was more subtle than the one before, which meant each movement was less, so that by the time he had gotten through the two truckloads and the one boat that had come in for support, even Remo could hardly tell the movements.

Toward the end, the point was to make the bodies fall in a pattern. Remo did not notice the attackers seemed to be parts of units. He told Chiun to save a few for information.

"How many?"

"Three," said Remo.

"Why three, when one is enough?"

"If they're American, two of them won't know what they are doing here."

Chiun saved three stunned groggy men who could not believe such a frail wisp of a man had done such damage. One of them had a vicious scar across his cheek. They tried to focus on the one boat that remained on the river. But it was not easy for the three battered men to spot their potential rescuers. The boat had fled.

"Come with us. We'll talk to you later," said Remo.

"You are going to bring prisoners before an emperor?" said Chiun.

"I want to talk to them."

"One does not bring prisoners before an emperor unless the emperor requests it."

"Another damned king," said the man with the scar on his face.

Remo pushed them along through the gates of Folcroft. Apparently, since no shots were fired, no one inside knew of the mayhem outside. Nurses and patients went about their business in orderly routine, the perfect cover for a secret organization, a lunatic asylum.

They went through the main entrance and then up three flights of stairs. The prisoners looked around to see if they might escape, but Remo's reassuring smile changed their minds. The smile said that Remo would be pleased for them to try it. They didn't.

"What do you mean by another king?" asked Remo.

"Kings are lunatics. We know. We're working for one now. This guy has been holding tryouts all week. He says he is looking for his king's champion."

"Spanish," said Chiun. "They have champions to fight battles. They are not true assassins, but the best fighters."

"Yeah. Well, our team won. We wiped out a Burmese SWAT team, three Ninja groups, and a South American enforcer for drug smugglers. And now look at what we run into."

"The majors," said Remo, guiding them a bit faster.

Smith's outer door was closed. The secretary who guarded that door typed efficiently while looking at a sheaf of papers. Like many secretaries she actually ran the entire organization. This left Smith to run CURE. She of course did not know about his other business. Dr. Smith to her was just another executive who dealt with higher matters.

Smith could be dead behind those doors, and she would not know it until they eventually broke through the doors. Then they would find the body. By then all the computer information about crime in America would have been dispersed to different enforcement agencies, and the organization would no longer exist. There would be no more files, no more access to them, no more service.

"I've come to see Dr. Smith," said Remo.

"Dr. Smith only sees people by appointment."

"I have one."

"That's impossible. He doesn't have an appointment this month."

"He forgot. Ask him. He does," said Remo.

The secretary looked at the three men, one nursing a broken arm. She looked at Chiun, imperiously satisfied with himself. She looked at Remo in a pair of slacks and a T-shirt.

"Well, all right," she said. She buzzed inside. Remo waited. There was no answer. She buzzed again.

Remo would give it ten more minutes. If Smith did not answer by then, he would just leave, maybe finish out this last assignment, but just walk away and leave Smith to be found the way he had planned.

"I'm sorry, he's not answering," said the secretary.

"I guess not," said Remo, and silently said good-bye to a good commander and a patriot.

He nodded the three men back toward the hallway. Then the door to Smith's office opened. The lemony face peered out.

"Come on in. Why were you waiting?" said Smith.

"Your secretary buzzed you," said Remo. "You didn't answer."

"I wasn't buzzed," said Smith.

"I did, Dr. Smith. Three times. You know, I think it didn't work. I've never had to buzz you before."

"We'll have to get it fixed."

"The last time I used it was twelve years ago when your wife Maude was here."

"Come on in, Remo, Chiun," said Smith.

"I'll be with you in a minute. I want to talk to these people. Do you have any empty rooms?" asked Remo.

"We have padded rooms," said Smith. "Take the patients there. See what they want. Then I am sure we can transfer them elsewhere."

"Oh Emperor Smith, our hearts ring in gratitude that we have come in time to save your glory that it may go down in ages henceforth," said Chiun.

The secretary looked to Dr. Smith.

"Outpatient," said Smith, and shut the door.

In the padded cell Remo found out more about the man who considered himself a king. His name was Harrison Caldwell. He had an estate in New Jersey. And he held shoot-outs, knife-outs, and combat drills in an effort to find the best man to be his "sword," his "champion."

"Whydya do it?" asked Remo.

"Why?" The man with the scar laughed. So did the others. "Do you know what he pays? He gives out gold bars like they're trinkets. The champion gets a chest of gold every month. He's the richest man in the world. Gold everywhere."

Chiun heard this and covered his breast with his frail parchmentlike hand.

"And pray tell, just where exactly does his Majesty live?" asked Chiun.

"We're not going, little father," said Remo.

"A king who pays in gold. An assassin waits for years to find the proper king and you just dismiss him. Talk to him. At least talk to him. Speak to the man. Do not be so rash."

"I've got work here."

"For the lunatic."

"Hey, what's going on?" asked the man with the scar. As Remo and Chiun left, Chiun was still pleading. Just speak once to the man. Just once. That was all Chiun asked. If, after talking to the king, Remo said no, then no it would be. After all, it was not like leaving America. New Jersey was part of America even if America wasn't all that happy about it.

Remo locked the door of the padded cell behind him. Several large orderlies appeared in the hallway.

"Dr. Smith said there are three criminally insane here. That the room?"

Remo nodded.

"You're lucky you got out of there alive. Those guys are going to be separated from the world for life," said the orderly.

"I'm a doctor. I know how to handle these things."

"Dr. Smith said they killed the last two doctors who tried to treat them."

"But not us," said Remo.

The orderlies unfolded three straitjackets and entered the padded room.

"All I ask is a single introduction, a mere hello. Just to speak to this king," said Chiun.

"No," said Remo.

"Then there is nothing I can do with you, Remo. I have saved you once and saved you again, all without thanks. I cannot take this anymore. I must go where I am respected. Good-bye."

"Where are you going?"

"To the king who knows the value of an assassin. If he pays such dolts as the ones we have locked up, can you imagine the gold he will shower on Sinanju?"

"What are you going to do with all that gold?"

"Replace that which was stolen, restock that which you would not help me recover. That is what I will do for a start."

By the time Remo got to Smith's office, Chiun was long gone. Remo was feeling somewhat angry, definitely disturbed, and not too sure of what he wanted to do.

He was glad Smith was alive, even if he talked incessantly about the incredible compromise of all the bodies strewn from coast to coast and his plan to move the organization from Folcroft to a large bank in midtown Manhattan. Suddenly Smith's tribulations seemed like small talk to Remo.

"Who were those men?" asked Smith.

"There is a lunatic who thinks he is a king, named Harrison Caldwell. Lives on an estate in New Jersey. Has people fighting to the death to win a position from him."

"Caldwell. The name has come up. Why does he want us?"

"I don't know."

Smith punched the name and a code into his computer terminal. Caldwell, Harrison, indeed had a record in the organization's files. Somehow, quite suspiciously, this man had amassed an incredible fortune—enough of a fortune to build his own little country within a country. He also got rich much too quickly—even for a gold digger. CURE kept track of these quick fortunes.

"He's a bullionist," added Smith.

"I think he's making gold. I think he's the one. It's done with uranium."

"Then he's the one who's stealing it," said Smith.

"Exactly," said Remo.

"And guess who has just been appointed chairman of the Nuclear Control Agency."

"The fox in charge of the henhouse," said Remo.

"Well, I think that explains why he could conduct such an incredibly complex campaign to track us down. He has the money to do it.

"Remo, I think it would be good if you took care of this matter, now."

"Okay," said Remo, but there was hesitation in his voice.

''Anything wrong?''

''No,'' said Remo, who was wondering how he would take on Chiun. He had never begged Chiun before and he wasn't sure begging would work now.

13

In the court of Harrison Caldwell Chiun found true and perfect happiness. The man accepted the Oriental's laudations and tributes of voice. And he responded with gold, promising to ship, or to lay it before Chiun in a vast pile.

There were, of course, a few amateur assassins to be proven imcompetent, but that was no trouble. The breath of lotus blows took care of them and the lotus variation, always a favorite with Westerners who liked to see hands move, pleased the king greatly.

But this king said he had known of Chiun, if not by name then by deed. For did he not have a white partner recently? Chiun answered, indeed he did, and that to work for a wise king like Harrison Caldwell meant a long life.

For this king was the very man whose face had appeared on television, calling for an end to random violence. And Chiun had always believed this was just the sort of man who would appreciate a great assassin.

The king even supplied an elegant little chair for Chiun. And all of this—the gold, the chair, the honor—came before Chiun even had a chance to look around. But who had to look around? One knew royalty when one saw it.

And then Remo came, rudely came. He barged right into the throne chamber, pushing aside guards.

"We see your partner has come," said His Majesty Harrison Caldwell.

"We will both serve you," said Chiun. "Two are better than one."

"I will not," said Remo. He hadn't even bowed to His Majesty. He stood there in his slacks and T-shirt, his hands on his hips, uncouth beyond reason, an embarrassment to the House of Sinanju.

Chiun rose quickly from his special stool. He pushed his way through several courtiers and got Remo into a corner.

"Are you mad?" he hissed. "This is a king, a real king, with real gold, and real tribute. He even has a chair for his assassin. Keep your peace. Let us enjoy decent work for once. See how it is to be well-treated."

"Have you looked around?"

"I see all I need to see."

"Have you looked at his standards?"

"We are here to defend them, not gaze upon them."

"Ask him for your gold now."

"I wouldn't insult him."

"You always said that getting the money in advance was the sign of a true assassin. Let's see his gold."

Chiun turned to Caldwell, who had motioned everyone else aside so he could watch the two. With a great bow, Chiun said he had been arguing with his assistant.

"Not knowing great kings, your Majesty, my friend foolishly doubted thy awesome grandeur. Would you show him how foolish he is by showing him the tribute that I know abounds here?"

"It will be our pleasure," said Harrison Caldwell. With that, he ordered up his special family engraved bullion, in special two-hundred-pound bars, the crest emblazoned in the center of each.

Then he sat back triumphantly even as Remo stared angrily at him. He asked the younger man why he showed such anger to a king who only wished to please.

"Because my teacher, whom I respect and love, has made a beginner's mistake, one he knows not to make," said Remo.

"And what is that?" asked Caldwell. He felt truly safe now. He could enjoy his throne and expand its boundaries, and no one would ever stop him again. Nor would he have to resort to poisonings or even lying. He would merely have to dispatch his two assassins, men trained to appreciate true royalty. The younger, of course, would take a while to learn. But the gold would be a good teacher.

"When one's emotions are too strong, one does not see things he should. My father will see everything very soon."

The blare of horns announced the arrival of the gold, but Remo didn't need to hear them. He could feel it as it passed through the doors, stacked bar upon bar, gold pyramids on trolleys. He was sure Chiun would also.

But Chiun just stood his ground, a respectful distance from the throne. Finally Remo said:

"Look at the markings, little father, not at your hopes for our wealth. Look at what is here."

Chiun glanced imperiously at Remo and then with smooth gliding steps moved to the gold. He glanced at the glittering stack, then turned to thank the king. But when he looked again, when he saw the markings on the gold, he stopped. It was then that he began to be aware of the room. He looked around at the standards hanging from the wall.

He had seen it. The apothecary jar on the center of the crest.

"Is this your family crest?" asked Chiun.

"For centuries," said Caldwell.

"So you thought you were safe to try it again," said Chiun.

Caldwell could not believe what he saw. The usually extremely polite Oriental did not even bow as he approached the throne.

"You there, where are your manners?" said Caldwell. He was not going to lose control of the man now.

Chiun did not answer.

"Stop," ordered Caldwell.

Chiun did not stop.

Nor did Chiun kiss the hand of King Caldwell. He slapped him across the face. Not even as a boy had Harrison Caldwell felt the insult of a slap across the face.

And then there was another.

"Adulterer. See now, world, what happens to him who adulterates an assassin's tribute," announced Chiun.

And Caldwell felt himself yanked from the throne and beaten around the room like a dog who has fouled the wrong place. The courtiers fled in panic. Chiun brought Caldwell to the cursed gold, placed his head on it, and sent head and soul to the place of the man's cheating ancestors.

"They never learn," said Chiun.

"I think he knows now," said Remo.

Before they left, they released the prisoners who were shackled in the dungeon. Some of them were losers in the combats Caldwell had staged. One of them was a woman. Consuelo Bonner.

She was surprised to see Remo up and about, and guessed that Chiun saved him.

"Again," said the Master of Sinanju wearily.

ABOUT THE AUTHORS

WARREN MURPHY has written eighty books in the last twelve years. His novel *Trace* was nominated for the best book of the year by The Mystery Writers of America and twice for best book by The Private Eye Writers of America. *Grand Master*, co-written with his wife Molly Cochran, won the 1984 Edgar Award. He is a native and resident of New Jersey.

RICHARD SAPIR is a novelist with several book club selections. He is a graduate of Columbia University and lives with his wife in New Hampshire.

⊘